Elizabeth Bennett lives near New York City but does not have leisurely afternoons.

The Afternoons
of a Woman
# of Leisure

Elizabeth Bennett

SPHERE

First published in the United States of America in 1993 by Blue Man Books
First published in Great Britain in 1993 by Warner
Reprinted 1993, 1994 (twice), 2001
Reissued by Sphere in 2012
This editioin published in 2013

A CIP catalogue record for this book
is available from the British Library.

ISBN 978-0-7515-5119-8

Typeset in Sabon by Hewer Text UK Ltd, Edinburgh
Printed and bound in Great Britain by Clays Ltd, St Ives Plc

Papers used by Sphere are from well-managed forests
and other responsible sources.

MIX
Paper from
responsible sources
FSC® C104740

Sphere
An imprint of
Little, Brown Book Group
100 Victoria Embankment
London EC4Y 0DY

An Hachette UK Company
www.hachette.co.uk

www.littlebrown.co.uk

The Afternoons of a
Woman of Leisure

PART ONE

A Woman of Leisure

Chapter One

Joanna is a woman of leisure. She knows this for a fact because, in the two years since she married Curtis, she has had nothing to do in the afternoons. Their shingled house, technically in the suburbs of the city but perched on a sandy bluff above the shore, lets in salty breezes and light and seems to require little cleaning. Curtis likes bare things: wooden floors, uncluttered surfaces, a lack of frills around windows. Curtis is also the acknowledged cook in the household, and every evening he returns from the city with a cut of something or a limb of something else and drifts into the kitchen like a ghost in the place it has always lived. Joanna, sitting out on the porch, hears first chopping and the clatter of pots being taken down, then smells, invariably, something rich and inviting. He likes to cook for her, she knows. He likes to remove the smells of money and office politics from his hands by dipping his fingers into spices and flour and the softness of ripe vegetables.

Curtis is many years older than Joanna, who is nearly twenty-eight, and Joanna is not his first wife. Curtis's first wife was his own age, a reportedly small and aggressive woman who was made wealthy by their divorce. She now lives in the city and apparently runs some kind of lucrative business from her penthouse east of the park. She is not a woman of leisure, Joanna knows, and Joanna wonders what her afternoons must be like. She imagines the ringing of telephones and the clatter of fax machines, the rushed dressing for lunch and dinner appointments. Joanna thinks often of Curtis's other wife, whom she has never met. Sometimes, and more and more frequently over these past few months, she has tried to imagine what their lovemaking must have been like, but the only image she can conjure is of bouncing beneath covers, the tops of two curly heads barely visible at one end of the bed.

Joanna's own hair is not curly. Curtis calls it gossamer hair, and it is pale blond, unbleached and pure. When she takes it down from its customary knot at the back of her neck, it settles in wisps over her breasts and the pink of Joanna's nipples peeks through. Again and again, Joanna has performed this strange and private ritual during her afternoons, while Curtis is away at work, first removing her sweater then reaching behind her back to unhook the lace bra with a flick of her hand, then pulling the bronze colored metal pins from her hair and easing it down over her skin. Then she backs up and sits on the edge of the bed and watches herself in the full-length mirror mounted on the closet door. Just watches.

Sometimes, as she sits at the foot of the bed, a stronger breeze comes through the screened window and lifts the hair again, revealing not only the pink of the nipple but its point, suddenly hard as the cold brushes over it. Joanna takes her breast in her hand and tests that hardness with the tips of her fingers, and a current runs through her at the touch, sinking to the soles of her feet like melting water, then shooting upward again, gathering damply in her crotch. At these moments, she feels herself to be at the edge of understanding something important, something unique to herself, something Curtis has neither explained nor even intimated. Joanna would like to know what it is, but when Curtis holds her it is in the manner of a father holding a child, snug in his lap, her head settled in the crook of his neck.

This is why Joanna is sometimes tempted to telephone Curtis's first wife, despite the fact that they are strangers. She would like to ask her about the bouncing figures underneath the blanket, and whether Curtis ever held her snugly on his lap, his broad hands warm on her thighs over her skirt. She would also like to ask whether Curtis, during his first marriage, kissed his wife tenderly on her forehead before going to bed in his own room at the end of the hall. Joanna is fairly certain that he did not. After all, Curtis's first marriage produced a son, now as old as Joanna, or perhaps even a little older. Joanna has never met him, either.

They have not always been exactly chaste, however. At first, Curtis turned to her often at night, late, almost in sleep. His lovemaking was baffling to Joanna, ethereal, directed by some hidden authority within her husband and always leaving her wanting something just beyond her reach, something she couldn't quite identify. But slowly even those hushed and dark encounters became fewer and fewer, breezier, more breath-less, more brief. Now Curtis only touches her in fond appreciation of her beauty: a finger tracing the softness of her cheek, a kiss to the back of her hand, a breath exhaled into the pale gold of her hair. One night, not long ago, she followed him to his bedroom and stood in the doorway, her thin nightgown fluttering at her ankles. Curtis sat up in bed.

'I was wondering,' Joann had said. 'I mean, about this.' She gestured at the room. Curtis was silent. 'It's just,' she said finally, 'that I miss you. I miss your touching me.'

Curtis motioned to her and she padded softly to the edge of his bed and sat down. His hand found her knee and settled there. 'You're very beautiful,' he told her, his voice strange and low in the dark room. 'It's a funny time for me. I'm not in my prime anymore, but I'm not old yet. I don't know how things will settle, but I'd like it if you stayed with me.' Joanna watched the shadow of his face. 'Call it a phase,' Curtis said finally. 'It may not last much longer.'

'Okay,' Joanna said, getting up.

Curtis turned over and went immediately to sleep, even as she watched by the side of his bed. As if, she thought later, they had been discussing nothing more important than the groceries they needed or their plans for a Sunday. Slowly, she felt her way along the wall and closed the door behind her. Back in her own bedroom, she carefully pulled her sweater over her head and reached back to release the bra, then picked the bronze pins from the knot at the back of her neck. The lights were off. Joanna had never done this at night, and now she felt rather than saw the hardening of her nipples under the soft shifting of hair. She closed her eyes and, when she did, blood seemed to pulse in her breasts, darkening their points, so Joanna imagined, to a deep red. She peeled off her skirt and leaned back on the bedspread, feeling its ridges beneath her back.

A phase, he had said. Her own fingers inched beneath the lace rim of her underwear, nesting in the soft and now damp hairs mounded there. Instinctively, the muscles of Joanna's thighs relaxed and parted. Her fingers slipped and slid into the warmth at the center of her body. With her other hand she reached for her breast and stroked it, testing the point, the stiffness of it. Her underwear gathered in the fold between her buttocks and Joanna arched against its tightness until the urge to strain was replaced with a numbness and a vague sense of loss and she relaxed. She had not come, exactly. Joanna had never actually had an orgasm, she believed, but she knew that whatever passion was within herself had barely been touched by her lovemaking with Curtis or her lovemaking alone. Curtis wasn't the only one with a sense of fleeing time, she thought then, reaching down for a blanket to cover herself in the cool darkness. Joanna's sigh filled the still room. It was time for a phase of her own. And now, before it was too late.

Chapter Two

One Tuesday early in the summer, after Curtis has left for his office, Joanna dresses for the city herself. She puts on stockings, the kind with underwear sewn into them, a slip and a skirt, a lace bra, high heels and a white sweater. The day is warm and bright as she drives to the train station, and already she feels moisture begin to gather beneath her arms. She has not thought to put on deodorant, but before she leaves the car she reaches under her sweater and sprays perfume between her breasts, then inhales approvingly.

The train is full of women, sleek and groomed, their short hair tamed further by clips and hairbands. They hold their pocketbooks firmly in their laps as if they were small animals who might jump down at any moment. Joanna imagines that each of these women is on her way into the city to meet a lover in a hotel room downtown. For a moment she wonders whether she should abandon her own rather vague plans and follow one of them instead, but when the train finally pulls into the downtown station the women quickly disperse, and Joanna takes the escalator to street level and gets into a waiting taxi.

The city swelters in the summer heat, and tempers run high. Twice Joanna's taxi driver leans out of his window to hurl curses at other drivers and passers by. To Joanna he offers only low mutters in another language. Farther uptown, the traffic thins and they begin to move faster, twisting aggressively through the streets until they reach the park. 'Here,' Joanna says suddenly, leaning forward. It is not quite the address she had given him, but it is close enough. She pays him and gets out.

The Afternoons of a Woman of Leisure

Joanna walks along the edge of the park for another block and finally takes a seat on the bench. The bench faces the canopied apartment building where Curtis's first wife now lives. It is nearly twelve o'clock. She does not know how long she will wait here, or even exactly what she is waiting to see. Joanna decides to wait until something happens, to then get up and find something else to do. It sounds simple enough. People glance at her as they walk past, the women with distrust or dismissal, the men with interest. One hesitates, does a shuffle step, then apparently thinks better of it and walks on. Joanna begins to wish that she had brought some sort of a prop to explain her presence: a newspaper, a book, a sketchpad.

A brisk movement makes her look up. Curtis's first wife is standing beneath the canopy of her apartment building, talking with the uniformed doorman. Joanna recognizes her from a photograph which Curtis still keeps in his own bedroom, right beside a picture of Joanna. The woman is short and curvaceous with wildly red hair curling to her shoulders. She nods when the doorman speaks to her, her hands on her hips. She is wearing a short black dress, linen, Joanna thinks, and flat black shoes. She turns and walks purposefully down the street, and abruptly Joanna gets up and begins to follow her, careful not to catch up with her own longer stride.

Curtis's first wife walks away from the park and turns south on a shady, shop-lined avenue. She is carrying a leather briefcase which must be heavy, Joanna thinks, because the woman frequently shifts it from hand to hand. She pauses frequently to peer into shop windows, and Joanna stops too, a few windows back, trying to look interested in the merchandise. Her body seeps beneath the white sweater, and one of her toes has begun to rub against the leather of her high-heeled shoe. Suddenly, Curtis's first wife ducks into a restaurant and crisply closes the door behind her. Joanna hesitates for a moment, then, remembering her earlier mistake, goes to a newsstand on the corner and buys a magazine. She rolls it in her hand and enters the same restaurant, taking a seat by the window.

Inside, the air is beautifully cool. The flowers on her table move slightly in the air from an overhead fan. A waiter brings her a menu and Joanna studies it for a moment before asking for a glass of white wine and a salad. Then she unrolls her magazine and slowly, surreptitiously, looks around.

Curtis's first wife is seated across the room at a small table with a stunning black woman. Both are reading menus. The black woman wears a red, clinging shirt that bares her upper chest and much of her shoulders. She is tense, Joanna thinks. When Curtis's first wife turns to her she visibly quivers, but the question is apparently about food because they both turn back to their menus with seemingly increased interest. After the waiter leaves with their order, the black woman glances nervously around the room. Joanna pretends to read her magazine.

She sips her wine. The two women talk, leaning slightly towards each other, as if they don't want their conversation overheard. The black woman nods, her arms crossed protectively over her breasts. Curtis's first wife reaches into her briefcase and removes a pad and a calculator. The other woman watches as her hand moves briskly down the page, writing figures, Joanna thinks. She uses the back of her pen to punch buttons on the calculator and holds it up to show the result to the black woman, then the calculator is put away. The two women barely touch their lunch. Curtis's first wife is smiling. Frequently, she pats the arm of the black woman, familiarly, comfortingly. Then, without warning, they rise to go. Joanna had not noticed the arrival of their check, and now hurriedly signals for her own. Curtis's first wife opens her purse and hands the other woman a small white card which the black woman takes and slips into a pocket of her skirt. Joanna's check has not arrived, and her frustration builds as she helplessly watches the two women leave, one holding the door for the other. As they pass by her window, however, something happens. Something unexpected. The white card falls silently from the black woman's pocket and flutters to the sidewalk, unnoticed. When she presses her face to the glass, Joanna can see it lying there, pure white on the grey of the pavement, a spattering of black writing on its surface. Her heart leaps. By the time she looks up, the two women have gone.

Outside, a few minutes later, she bends to it and it comes to her hand as if it belonged there. In the middle of the card is a single capital letter: 'O'. Beneath that is a phone number. Joanna puts the card carefully into her purse then, stepping to the curb, raises her arm to signal an approaching taxi.

Chapter Three

The train is crowded, this time with men who are leaving work early. As they pull out of the station and into the labyrinth of paths beneath the city, a loudspeaker crackles to life and informs them that there will be no air conditioning due to work along the line. There may also, the speaker says, be some short delays.

There is a collective groan. The bald man seated next to Joanna shakes and refolds his newspaper then loosens his tie, releasing a puff of odor. Joanna waits for a polite minute before getting up. She makes her way through the car, steadying herself with her hands along the tops of the seats. Just before the door she miscalculates the motion of the train and her hand settles not on a seat but on the back of a brown head. When she turns back briefly to apologize, Joanna meets a pair of steel-colored eyes in a pale, oblong face. 'Sorry,' she murmurs. The man nods. She continues walking but, even then, Joanna can feel those eyes following her the rest of the way.

In the small space between cars, Joanna finds room to stand next to a slightly opened window. The air rushing in is not cool, but it isn't unpleasantly hot, either. She leans against the wall and crosses her arms, trying to drift.

The train rises above ground and picks up speed, crossing the no man's land between the outer edge of the city and the inner edge of the suburbs. The buildings here are burned out and boarded up. They rise between lots of rubble and sporadic trees. Leaning over towards the window, she can see the first of two long tunnels between the city and the suburbs approaching swiftly, but just before they enter it the train halts for a work crew and sits baking on the track for them to finish. Joanna wipes her face and breathes deeply. Finally, the train starts again and enters the blackness. Behind her, there is a shuffle, a pause and a click. Someone has entered the bathroom. Outside the window, darkness flies by.

On the other side of the tunnel the houses have small, fenced-in plots of grass and concrete. Joanna catches a fleeting glimpse of a child, playing with a rubber ball. She closes her eyes again. The second tunnel, she remembers isn't far beyond the first.

But as soon as they enter it the train begins to slow again, then only to crawl. Finally they stop entirely and the loudspeaker cracks and says, merely, 'Sorry, folks. This'll be a minute.'

It's very dark. Joanna holds her hand before her face and can barely make it out. She is glad that she left her seat. She does not like the idea of being in total darkness in a room full of strangers. Here at least, she's alone. Except for the man in the bathroom, she thinks as its door clicks open, reminding her.

There is another shuffle, then stillness. Perhaps he's decided to wait it out too, she thinks, but even as she thinks it there is a small wind at the nape of her neck. Joanna freezes, her eyes open, staring at nothing. The man takes another step and comes up, lightly, behind her. Then, except for his breathing, there is nothing: no word, no touch.

She is astonished at her own calmness, for which there is no rational explanation. Surely this is, to say the least, an inappropriate contact and an uninvited one. And yet, Joanna knows instinctively that the body standing behind her means her no harm. It's warm against her back. It's still. It's simply *there*.

And suddenly, without warning, she wishes it *would* move. She would like to feel those unseen hands beneath her clothing, against her skin, even, she realizes, inside her body. Joanna's throat catches at the thought, releasing a small gasp. The body behind her is motionless. What is he waiting for?

she thinks but even as the words form in her mind, Joanna knows the answer. He's waiting for permission. Not an involuntary gasp, something deliberate and unmistakable, something that could only mean yes.

Joanna closes her eyes and slowly arches her body, carefully, until her head falls slightly back and her buttocks first touch and then press firmly into the stiffness in his groin. Immediately, his hands come up and press her head between them, the mouth at her neck opens and seems to swallow her nape, making her shiver. She presses back harder and he moans, a low sound that vibrates into her skin.

The hands descend either side of her head and reach in front of her, moving lightly over her breasts and stomach, then coming back to find the nipples, already hard and pressing against his fingers. Instinctively, she pulls at her own sweater, gathering it into damp fists, and he dives beneath it, his hands broad and warm on her abdomen. Behind her, she senses his urgency and reaches back, finding the thick outline of his cock and offering it her hand. The man moans again, and Joanna feels the rush of her own power, and smiles to herself.

His fingers are raking her breasts, side to side. They pull at the lace, making small tears, then, frantic, they tear deliberately and Joanna feels herself falling into his hands. The tongue licks her neck. Her nipples are his now, rubbed between fingers, teased and brushed. Joanna squeezes the stiffness in her hand. A voice says, 'Lift your skirt.'

She bends down and does what he asks, wadding it in front of her, the back of her stockinged legs now bare, then turns until she almost faces the wall and leans slightly forward. Briefly, the man steps away from her, then Joanna hears the rasp of his fly coming undone, a quick catch in his breath as he releases himself. A hand reaches for her ass, then another, then both dip between her parted thighs and are instantly wet. She moves her hips slightly, rubbing against them. Her nipples, crushed against the wall, throb with heat. He is impatient with her stockings, would like to tear them, Joanna thinks.

She frees one of her own hands and reaches back to show him the edge at her waist, where it begins, and he grabs it, rolling it with both palms down the sides of her legs to mid-thigh. She arches back to him, separating her buttocks, inching her legs farther apart, wanting his wet hand, his slippery fingers inside her. Instead the man's hands settle on her ass, softly at first and then more insistently. She is being spread apart, wide and wider, until she feels tightness and something just short of pain. There is a shift of his weight behind her, then something shocking and cold. He is kneeling at her feet, hands parting her behind, licking her slowly. Joanna presses her mouth to the wall and its steel swallows away the sounds she makes. The tongue is determined and slow and sweet. It dips into her and out of her, lapping the slit from front to back and pausing at her anus, poking inside with its tip. Joanna reaches back to hold him there for a long moment, her fingers twisting in soft curls. She wonders, oddly what color they are. The man breathes warm air into her.

Come on, Joanna thinks. She has not said it aloud but the man rises anyway, his pelvis tilted beneath hers, and one arm snakes around her waist. She offers her hand as a guide but he doesn't need it. Joanna feels the thrust in his moan even before she feels it inside her, but then she fills with him and moans herself. It is a slow, sweet pounding, a softening, a secret thing. She reaches for her own breasts, imagining invisible mouths at them. A hand tangles in her pubic hair, looking for something and then finding it, pressing gently at the rim of each of his thrusts. The movement quickens. Her cunt feels swollen, sticky, open. His gasps sound like agony.

The word in her mind is 'almost,' and she thinks it over and over, 'almost . . . almost . . .' but before she can reach it he comes, hissing a low 'fuck' into her ear like a message in a game of Telephone, filling her with quick, searing heat. 'Fuck,' the man says again, this time to no one in particular, a twinge of mourning in his voice. He sighs and leans against her, briefly.

Then the hand slips quickly away and is busy behind her. She feels him falling free of her cunt in a moist wave and hears the rustle and zip of his clothing. For a moment he is motionless, then Joanna senses his hand brushing past her and along the wall. He moves away and she remains still, her cheek to the cool metal. The heavy door into the passenger car is wrenched open and closed. She can't hear his footsteps on the other side of it.

A minute more, she doesn't move. Then, dimly, Joanna is aware of her rolled pantyhose biting the outer sides of her thighs. She sighs and reaches down to roll them up again, pausing to lightly brush the mound of her pubic hair through the scratchy surface of the stocking. It throbs and quivers with urgency, but now it is too late. Her skirt is released and falls heavily around her knees. Joanna tries to adjust the torn lace of her bra over her tender nipples, then pulls down her sweater. Automatically, her hands reach up to test the knot of her hair. It is smooth and untroubled.

Her mood is stunned but calm and almost, she realizes, tender. The train gives a shudder, then another, then slowly begins to rock forward. Joanna leans down for her bag and fumbles inside for a compact. The lights flip on, stunningly bright. When her eyes adjust, the first thing she sees is her own face in the small mirror, lips pursed, smiling, the eyes full of mirth. She is thinking, so this is how it begins.

Chapter Four

That night, during dinner Joanna ponders her curious day: the women on the morning train, Curtis's first wife and the beautiful black woman in intimate conference at the restaurant, the plain white card with its inexplicable 'O' on the pavement, her strange, potent encounter in the train. All evening, she has expected some recognition from Curtis, some curious glance, an insinuating 'What did *you* do today?'

But Curtis has asked her nothing, said nothing, done nothing out of the ordinary. His talk, over the meal, is of his own day at the large and distinguished bank where he serves as president, a position he has held since his father died and vacated the same job. Curtis has both inherited and made an enormous amount of money, some of which, Joanna now realizes, has probably made its way into 'O', whatever 'O' is, via his divorce settlement with his first wife. He was generous with his money then, as he is generous now, with Joanna. But although Joanna is free to spend Curtis's wealth, her monetary demands have always been sparse: clothing and books, a new car when the Ford she drove before her marriage died of old age. And now, of course, the money isn't relevant. After all, what she wants (what she *needs*, Joanna corrects herself) can't be bought.

Or can it? Joanna wonders. Smiling to herself, she imagines a full-page ad in the daily paper: Woman of Leisure Seeks Sexual Fulfillment. Top Rates Paid.

But who would apply for such a position? She thinks, and what good would it do? She has no wish for a gentle lover to stroke her and coo at her and tell her how much he loves her. Curtis does that, Joanna knows, and still she has never had a climax. Even the man on the train failed to satisfy her, though there was something in that encounter which brought her close, closer than she had ever been in the past. What was it? she asks herself. She thinks of his 'Fuck' in her ear, the crude command to lift her skirt, the greed of his fingers at her crotch and is suddenly flushed and trembling. Something about that . . . Joanna thinks. It comes to her then that she would like to be taken, her pleasure imposed upon her. Not forced, exactly, but cornered, pressured, insinuated upon.

Without warning, a broad and shadowy land-scape seems to open before her, stretching between rape, which both terrifies and disgusts her, and the bonded, affectionate lovemaking of couples, which clearly bores her. She cannot distinguish the possibilities and scenarios between these extremes but, instinctively, Joanna senses that her own desires belong with them. She wishes she knew what to do next, how to find her way into that place. She wishes someone would tell her or, better yet, take her there. But how can she ask if she doesn't know, exactly, what she is asking for?

'Are you all right?' Says Curtis, interrupting her thoughts. 'You look a little stricken.'

'I'm fine,' Joanna says. He reaches across the table and refills her wine glass.

'Did you have a nice day?' She nods, smiling. 'Anything special?'

'The usual,' says Joanna.

'You are so sweet,' her husband says, kissing her hand.

Chapter Five

The next morning dawns sunny and hot. After Curtis has left, Joanna sits outside with her coffee, watching the ripple of sunlight on the water. Already, she has begun to perspire, a light mist over her forehead. Joanna sighs. As usual, she has nothing planned for the afternoon. The sun beats down, promising to get even hotter. A good day for the beach, Joanna decides. Might as well make the best of it.

Just before noon, she changes into her bathing suit, a white strapless one-piece that hugs her breasts and cuts high over her hips. Over it, she puts on a long beach dress, shapeless and easy. Joanna fills her canvas bag with soda, sandals, her sunglasses and a long towel. When she is ready, she gets into her car and starts to drive.

Although the suburb where Curtis and Joanna live is technically on the water, most of the waterfront is wooded and slightly rocky. The beaches are farther away, some miles up the coast. Joanna's favorite beach is a sandy inlet between dunes at the foot of a cliff. The climb down it is long and, accordingly, the many mothers who bring their children to the beach in the summertime find it tedious and tend to keep away. Joanna is hoping for privacy, but when she finally arrives, several other beachgoers have already staked their claims and are stretched out, reading and talking. Resigned, Joanna lays down her towel and pulls off her beach dress, sighing as the ocean breeze begins to cool her hot skin. She sits cross-legged on her towel and watches the ocean. The other beachgoers ignore her.

The sun climbs and swells. Joanna drifts, wishing she had thought to bring something to read. An hour passes, then another. Drowsy in the heat, she lies on her stomach. To rest, she thinks dreamily, not to sleep. I won't fall asleep, Joanna tells herself.

But she does, floating off on the sound of the waves, the moist sunlight. When she wakes, it is into a shadow cast over her face, an object between herself and the sun. She squints and turns.

A man is standing over her, a tall man with thick white hair and, curiously, a young face, unlined. He wears jeans and paint-spattered sneakers, a crisp white shirt. He is watching her intently.

Joanna sits up and holds her knees protectively against her chest. The man examines her frankly, without embarrassment, his hands in his back pockets. He seems not to acknowledge the fact that she is now awake. Joanna looks around, fearfully. They are alone. This man isn't a rapist, she thinks, trying to calm herself. She does not know how she knows this, but she senses its truth. Joanna lets herself look up at him. 'Can I help you?' she asks, politely.

'I think so,' he says. His voice is soft, slightly ironic. 'Will you please come with me?'

Her eyes widen. Her hands grasp her own legs tightly. The man hasn't moved. He watches her with interest. She should run, Joanna thinks. She should scream. Instead, she shocks herself by asking him his name.

He shrugs. 'Do I need one? Why don't you give me one.'

'Robert,' Joanna says. He nods.

'So. Will you please come with me?'

Slowly Joanna uncoils her legs and lies back, her hands behind her head. The man's eyes follow the motion of her body, the stretch of her long legs, the rising mound at her crotch, the hardening nipples pressing against her white bathing suit. She hears his breath begin to quicken slightly, but he doesn't move. Permission, she thinks, a little sourly.

Abruptly, Joanna gets up and slips on her dress. Robert calmly watches her gather her things then, when she is ready, he beckons for her to follow and begins to climb to the top of the cliff.

'This is my car,' Joanna says when they reach the parking lot. It is the only one left.

'Then we'll drive,' he says. 'It isn't very far.'

She lets him in and climbs into the driver's seat. He sits calmly, his hands on his knees, looking straight ahead. She wonders, briefly, if she is wrong to assume he will not hurt her. 'This way,' Robert indicates, impatient. Joanna starts the car and drives.

'There,' he says, almost immediately. Joanna pulls up in front of a small red beach house.

'Is this your house?' She asks.

'I use it,' he tells her simply. 'It's owned by a friend. Please come inside.'

Joanna gets out of her car and follows him. Inside the entryway, an open door reveals a floor covered with spattered drop clothes, squeezed tubes of paint and several coffee cans full of soaking brushes. 'I'm an artist,' Robert says, dismissively, beckoning.

She follows him upstairs and into a large bedroom. White curtains flutter at the window. A mattress lies on the floor, covered haphazardly with sheets and twisted blankets. He closes the door behind them and leans against it, his arms folded. He watches her thoughtfully. 'You're very pretty,' Robert says at last. 'I suppose you don't need to be told that.'

'No,' Joanna says. 'I don't.'

He nods. 'All right.' She waits for him to take her, but he doesn't move. 'All right,' he says again. Then: 'Would you like me to fuck you?'

'Christ,' Joanna says, exasperated. 'Why do you think I'm here? Just do it, don't ask me anything else.'

He walks over to her calmly. 'Undress me,' he whispers. 'Slowly.'

Joanna sighs and starts to unbutton his shirt. His chest is pale and muscled and covered with white hair. The contrast of the hair against his young skin is breathtaking, Joanna thinks, wanting to pull at it, wanting his arms to pull her against him. But Robert only stands, patiently, waiting for her to slip off the shirt. She reaches down to unzip him, pausing briefly to run her fingers over the warm lump of his cock and it jumps slightly at her touch. Joanna eases the jeans down over his small ass then returns to his waist for the white cotton underpants. Robert sighs as they slip down. She kneels and helps him step out of his clothes, kicking off the sneakers, then straightens up to look at him.

He is beautiful, she thinks. She thinks she has never seen anything so beautiful. Still he stands motionless, his weight on one leg, his cock long and slightly curved. At its tip, a drop of moisture glistens.

'Come,' he says softly, extending his hand. Joanna takes it and he pulls her down beside him onto the mattress. She kicks off her sandals. His hands run over her lightly, too lightly, Joanna thinks. She presses up against him but he only continues, barely making contact. She pulls off her beach dress, hoping the clinging bathing suit will excite him more but he seems not to notice. His cock rubs against her thigh, regularly but without intensity. He kisses her face softly, her cheeks and neck and shoulders.

Finally, deeply frustrated, Joanna yanks at her own bathing suit, pulling it down and wriggling out of it, flinging it away in disgust. Robert looks at her with mild interest, as if he is only pleasantly surprised to discover that there were breasts beneath the fabric, all this time. Tentatively, he touches them, brushing with his fingertips around the nipples but never over them. He licks softly between her breasts and down around her navel, but even his licks seem uncertain. 'Harder,' Joanna says, pleading, but he only looks up with slight curiosity. She sighs and looks away.

He is gentle between her legs, his fingers polite and sadly undemanding. Nonchalantly, he parts her thighs and enters her, lifting her ass as he pushes, his head on her chest. She feel the slippery rhythm of his thrusts, but only as if from a great distance. His breath, over her nipple, is mild and warm. Joanna feels nothing, but she is too resigned to the situation to actually resent it. She is just waiting for it to be over.

Robert comes, moaning, his face between her breasts. Joanna shifts impatiently. A waste, she is thinking. A waste of his beauty. A waste of her own desire. She can't wait to leave.

He rolls away from her and rests on his side, his chin perched on his elbow. Joanna lies still but says nothing.

'Thank you,' she hears him say. Then, matter of factly, 'You didn't come.'

'Of course not,' she spits at him, outraged. 'What did you expect?'

'I think,' Robert says, 'the question is, what did *you* expect.'

'I'm leaving,' Joanna says shortly. She starts to get up, but his hand suddenly shoots over and jerks her back by the shoulder, smacking her against the mattress. Robert grabs at her wrists and pins her, his face close to hers. He is staring at her. Joanna feels his thigh creep between her thighs, pressing upward, holding her down as she arches against it. Abruptly, she hears the rasp of her own breath and knows how much she wants him to pound her, to take her. When she looks into his face, he is smiling.

'I want you to come here tomorrow,' he says. There is a stiffness, a cruelty in his voice. 'At noon.'

'Why should I come back?' She sneers at him. His thigh presses her crotch and she moans, despite herself.

'Come back,' he says knowingly. 'I think you'll have a better time if you do.'

Robert shifts, letting her up. Furious, she grabs at her clothes and puts them on and leaves without another word. Outside, as she starts her car, Joanna looks up and catches sight of him in the upstairs window, laughing as he watches her go.

Chapter Six

Joanna's car pulls up to the red beach house, and stops. All during the previous night she has been haunted, tormented by the memory of Robert's thigh, pinning her to the mattress, his hands imprisoning her, the cruel edge in his voice. Still, she is not quite certain why she is here. Not to repeat what happened yesterday, Joanna thinks, firmly cautioning herself. If he touches her the same way today, she will simply leave and, this time, not return.

Joanna walks up to the front door. To her surprise, it is slightly open, swinging into the hallway. 'Hello?' She calls, but there is no answer. Cautiously, she pushes at the door and it swings into darkness. The shades, she thinks. All of the shades must be pulled. 'Hello?' She calls again, taking a step inside.

Suddenly, she is yanked and grabbed, a gloved hand clamped tightly over her mouth. Joanna struggles instinctively, twisting back against the body behind her, but it grips her hard and an unfamiliar voice calls her 'Bitch' and tells her to stop, immediately, or he will beat the shit out of her.

Joanna stops, breathing hard. Even through her terror, a part of her is smiling, glad that he knows, glad that he wants her this way. She is pressed against the wall, facing it. Hands tie a blindfold around her head. 'Don't move,' he tells her, starting to feel her, roughly but slowly, descending her sides as if he were searching for a weapon. The gloved hands pause at her heaving breasts, taking in the outline of the bra beneath her shirt, then move down Joanna's stomach to the top of her skirt. A hand lifts it from beneath and carefully feels between her legs, testing the dampness that already fills Joanna's underpants. She feels the skirt fall again.

'You're coming with me,' the voice says. 'Don't try to scream, or I'll hurt you. Understand?'

Shaking, Joanna nods. 'Please . . .' She starts to say but he seizes her mouth again.

'Don't bother,' he says. 'I'm going to do what I want with you.' He holds her hands together behind her back and pushes her a few steps forward, then turns her. 'Up,' he says. Joanna climbs. At the top of the staircase he pushes her sharply to the left. She feels a door open in front of her, then close behind. He turns her roughly around and presses her back, against a wall. A gloved hand glides over her neck and Joanna gasps.

Suddenly her wrist is seized, lifted to shoulder height and swiftly fastened to the wall. Then the other wrist. She pulls against the fastenings and feels leather chafing her skin. His breath is on her face and she senses his closeness. Then a fumble at the small of her back, the sound of a zipper, slowly coming undone. Joanna's skirt slips to her feet. 'Let's see what you look like,' he says quietly.

'No,' Joanna whimpers, and he laughs.

'Oh, but I think yes.'

Fingers unfasten the buttons of her shirt and she feels it come apart, exposing her bra, her belly, the upper edge of her underpants. Slowly, he moves the fabric aside and up, folding it behind her shoulders. A hand glides over her breastbone and slides up to casually cup her cheek. 'I'm going to fuck you so hard,' the voice confides, and Joanna moans.

He grabs her head and kisses her deeply, filling her mouth, roughly sucking her tongue. 'So hard,' he says again. Joanna pulls at her straps.

A hand creeps between her legs, fingering the damp fabric. She twists from it but it follows, slowly, gathering the cotton. 'You're wet,' the voice tells her, as if this is something she needs to be told. 'By the time I'm finished with you you'll be dripping, won't you?'

'No,' Joanna pleads, but his answer is the sound of tearing lace, his gloved hands ripping at the bra.

She hears his sigh as it comes apart and he pushes it aside, over her shoulders. The hands take frantic possession of her breasts, rubbing and pressing them then pinching the nipples between leather fingers.

'I'm going to suck your tits,' he informs her, then does, slowly, between his teeth. Joanna writhes, wild on the edge of pain. 'You love it, you little cunt,' he whispers, reaching behind her back to slide his hands firmly over her ass. She feels his cock, pressing through denim at her pubic bone where he thrusts, briefly, showing her his own stiffness and heat.

Then he sinks to his knees and smells her loudly, rubbing his nose between her sticky thighs. A mouth bites at her underwear and she feels the glide of his teeth taking it, pulling it slightly away and then letting it snap back. 'Oh, please,' Joanna moans. She hears the crackle of leather, then his gloves, falling to the floor. Warm fingers trace the upper line of her underwear, lifting it, then slowly, very slowly, inching it down, as if he were removing gauze from a wound. His warm breath plays in her pubic hair. Joanna presses her thighs together but he merely reaches between them, pulling the soaked cotton away until it falls at her feet.

For a moment, he is silent, his face at her crotch. Joanna breathes hard, open-mouthed. The heat in her cunt is maddening, tormenting. He blows, sending a sweet vibration through the hairs, then softly begins to lift them away with one finger, parting them over the crack, nudging them aside then lightly tracing the swollen lips. 'Spread your legs,' the voice says harshly, then, when she doesn't move, 'Do it, bitch, or I'll do it for you.'

Beneath the blindfold, Joanna is suddenly aware of her own tears. Gasping, she starts to inch her feet apart and his palms press her thighs impatiently. 'Wider,' he hisses. She tries to comply but he doesn't wait. Pushing her back against the wall, the hands spread her, stretching her cunt, opening her in front of his eyes. 'Nice,' the voice comments. 'Aren't you nice. You'd like me to lick you, wouldn't you?'

'No,' Joanna is sobbing, the blindfold drenched, her throat thick. 'Please don't do that.'

But he has already begun, first with the tip of his tongue, flicking softly at the base of her cunt, around the hole. Then the tongue flattens, gently coating the slick inner lips. Joanna becomes conscious of her own hips, tilting slightly against him. He laughs softly, then his mouth opens wide, swallowing her whole. She hears her own cry, deep and foreign as he sucks her, moving his face back and forth. Joanna pushes, rocking herself, feeling the pressure build and build. She knows it is about to happen, finally, his strong mouth pulling it out of her. 'Please,' she moans, and dimly, far away, a finger slowly enters her. Her muscles grab at it.

Suddenly, the mouth releases her and blows warmly, making her throb. 'You want to come in my face,' he comments quietly. The finger inside her is still. 'But you can't. I'm going to fuck you first. You'll come when I'm ready.'

He slips quickly out of her. Joanna hears the crackle of his zipper, the sound of denim folding, then the snap of elastic. He leans against her and reaches behind to lightly stroke her buttocks, touching the anus with curious fingers. Then, without warning, she is lifted from beneath, pressed back against the wall and finally, slowly, allowed to drop onto him. Now, for the first time, she is aware of his own sounds, a low moan at her ear. The cock seems to expand inside her, thickening and lengthening. She senses its curve. His hands clutch at her ass and he begins to move, rocking at first and then harder with long, beautiful thrusts. Joanna rubs against him, tightening her thighs at his hips, opening to each thrust. A mouth finds her breast, and sucks it, taking the nipple between teeth and licking it roughly. She starts to scream and he pounds still harder, quickening, then suddenly he is telling her now, come now, and she does, the love in his voice exploding through her cunt and thighs and breasts, shooting through her bloodstream like fire, and he fills her mouth with his tongue and bursts deep inside her, howling like something wild.

Chapter Seven

'Hush,' Robert croons, touching her face. Joanna cries freely, her sobs choked and loud. 'Hush,' he says again. Softly, he eases her down and she moans as he slips out of her. He lifts away the blindfold and she stares blankly at the dim room, then he reaches up to unstrap her wrists from the wall.

Without hesitation Joanna moves to hug him, clasping his shoulders and crying against his neck. His arms slide around her back and he holds her, his hands warm on her skin and comforting. 'It's okay,' he tells her, leaning against her. 'It's okay to cry.'

'Yes,' Joanna says thickly, her hands in Robert's white hair. A minute later, she looks him in the eye and says, 'That never happened to me before.'

'I should hope not!' He laughs, kissing her.

'No,' Joanna says. 'I mean, I never came before.'

He draws back slightly and studies her, his mouth serious. 'Well, well, well,' says Robert thoughtfully.

He takes her hand and leads her from the small, dark room and out into the hall to his bedroom. 'Let's lie down for a bit,' he says, settling her on the mattress then untwisting a blanket and folding it over them. Joanna settles her head on his white chest. Robert's cock rests wetly against her knee. She feels peaceful and sated, glad that she has finally begun to understand her own desires, and she wonders how he knew.

'Are you married?' He asks her suddenly, fingering the wedding and engagement rings on her finger.

'Yes,' Joanna says. 'Are you?'

'No,' says Robert. 'Are you happily married?'

'I don't know,' Joanna says truthfully. 'I've never really thought much about it. I guess I must be, or else I'd leave him.'

'Not necessarily,' he laughs. 'My parents were unhappily married for years, and they stayed married for far too long.'

'Can I ask you something?' Joanna says, shifting onto her elbow and looking at him. 'Why is your hair white? You look so young. How old are you, anyway?'

'Thirty,' he says. 'Actually, it's sort of private.' But then, seeing her disappointment, he shrugs. 'I saw something, when I was fifteen. It scared the shit out of me. I turned white overnight, and I've been that way since. Do you mind it?'

She shakes her head. 'It's beautiful. I think it's beautiful.'

Robert smiles, his hand behind his head. 'You're beautiful,' he says. 'And Christ, are you sexy.' Then he grows serious again. 'Unfortunately, I have to leave tomorrow.'

Joanna does not try to hide her disappointment. 'Where are you going?'

'Up north,' he says simply. 'There's an artist's colony where I spend my summers. I always do interesting work there, though sometimes,' he smiles, 'not quite what I plan to do before I go.'

'Oh,' Joanna says.

Later, he makes love to her again. Tenderly, like the day before, but this time with passion and Joanna responds. She slides down the mattress to lick his open thighs, gently rubbing his scrotum then filling her mouth with his cock, feeling its beautiful curve. He moans and pulls at her legs, parting them over his head and plunging his tongue inside her until she comes in a wave, sucking him in rhythm to her own contractions. When she has finished, she turns and lowers herself on his cock, one hand massaging his scrotum, the other reaching up to brush and pull the white hairs around his nipples. Robert bucks under her, the muscles of his stomach tight, his head whipping from side to side on the pillow. His climax is a thick eruption inside her and she groans at its heat, its power, his face contorted and flushed.

'I want to give you something,' he tells her afterwards, when she has dressed to go. He walks, naked, into another room and brings back a small white paperback which he puts directly into her bag. 'Something to read,' Robert says. 'I think you will enjoy it.'

'What is it?' Joanna asks, but he only smiles, silent. 'Does this mean I won't see you again?' She says.

'Oh, I think our paths may cross,' Robert tells her.

'Based on what?' says Joanna, a little hurt.

'On fate,' he says. 'I'm a great believer in fate. Fate,' he whispers, solemnly but with a sly grin, 'and destiny.'

Chapter Eight

The book is *The Story of* O. All the following day,
Joanna reads, entranced. She loves the lushness of
the writing, the sweet intensity of O's longing both
for love and punishment. And slowly, as she reads,
that shadowy landscape of Joanna's own desire
begins to fill with possibilities, scenarios, commands.
She would not like to be really hurt, she thinks, not
branded or pierced with irons. She is not sure she
would like to be whipped either, but she loves the
idea of the whip, its stiffness, the whistled flight it
would make through the air, descending, its crack

against her flesh. But not hurting, she tells herself. Not really hurting. What she wants is the taking of her own body, the probing of it, the possession of it by someone who makes her surrender. She wants, temporarily but completely, to belong to someone, to be without choice. O's problem, Joanna decides, is that she is in love with the man who forces and controls her and, accordingly, she is compromised, her will lost in servitude. If only, Joanna thinks, there could be a more balanced exchange, almost a business transaction! A way to be taken and used and then, when it is over, left alone to walk out the door.

As she reads, Joanna frequently sets the book aside and goes to her bedroom to masturbate, blissfully, always to a shattering climax. She wonders at her own former ineptitude, her inability to imagine these things for herself. As she comes, she thinks of Robert, pinning her spread-eagled against the wall, calling her 'cunt' and 'bitch', telling her how much she is going to like it, how hard he is going to fuck her. Joanna moans with happiness.

The Afternoons of a Woman of Leisure

When she finishes the book, late that afternoon, Joanna returns to her bedroom again, rubbing it between hands that smell lingeringly of her own cunt. She is about to hide the book in her bedside table when it occurs to her to check the name of the author again, so that she can ask at her bookstore for other works by the same person. When she turns to the title page, however, Joanna sees something she hadn't noticed before: a telephone number, written with a ballpoint pen. Its area code identifies it as a downtown exchange. Joanna stares at the number for a long time before reaching into her bag. Within her own mind, she is sure, but still she feels compelled to check, to convince herself of what she already knows. Mired in the chaos of her bag, she finally finds the small white business card and pulls it out, holding it next to the book. It is the same number.

The afternoon has grown dark. Joanna knows that Curtis will be home any minute. She sits silently in the shadowy room, thinking about the small but prosperous business run by Curtis's first wife in the city. Now, she imagines, she understands about the beautiful black woman, the intimacy of the conference she observed in the restaurant. 'O', Joanna thinks, rolling the single letter over her tongue. The simplicity of that is beautiful to her. 'O'.

Before she can stop herself, Joanna lifts the telephone and dials the number, gripping the receiver tightly in her hand. She breathes heavily, prepared to hang up, her body tense. After a pause, Joanna hears a whir of soft clicks, a hum, and then the purr of ringing. Once, twice, three times, and finally another click, loud and decisive.

On tape, a woman's voice says, 'This is the correct number for "O". You've reached an answering machine. The only rule by which we operate is, "All persuasions; no brutality." Think about that carefully. If it applies to you and your needs, you may leave a name and telephone number after the tone. Otherwise, there will always be someone here to answer at this number on weekday mornings between nine and eleven. Thank you for calling.'

The tone sounds, long and low. Softly, Joanna hangs up the telephone.

Chapter Nine

The following morning, after Curtis has left for the city, Joanna dials the number again. This time the phone is answered immediately. 'Yes,' the woman's voice says. It is a low voice, gravelly but soft and strangely peaceful.

'I would like to speak with O,' Joanna says.

'This is "O".' A pause, then, 'How may I help you?'

Joanna takes a breath. 'I think,' she says, 'I would like to work for you.' There is silence along the line.

'May I ask,' the woman says finally, 'whom you are working for now?'

'No one,' Joanna says. 'I would like to work for you.'

'I see.' Again, a long silence. 'How did you come to hear about us?'

For a moment, Joanna considers telling Curtis's former wife the truth, but the secret feels powerful to her, and she holds it in. 'From a man,' she says instead. 'I think, a client.'

'I see,' the woman says again. 'You know, we have a rule. "All persuasions, no brutality." Did you know that?'

'I knew,' says Joanna. 'I mean, I know. I understand.'

'And you are interested?'

'Yes.'

There is another pause. Joanna counts slowly to herself, breathing softly. 'We should meet,' the woman says at last. 'We should meet and talk about this.'

'Yes,' Joanna says.

'Next week, on Tuesday. For lunch. Will you meet me for lunch?'

'Yes,' Joanna says.

'What is your name?' The woman asks.

'Joanna,' says Joanna, without hesitation. Then, remembering herself, she adds, 'That isn't my real name. I mean that you may call me Joanna.'

'I understand,' the woman says calmly. 'You may call me Pauline. So . . . we will meet and talk, then?'

'Yes,' Joanna says.

'You will wear a red shirt or dress,' says Pauline, 'so that I will know you. You will wear no jewelry. You will sit with your hands folded on the tablecloth.'

'Yes,' Joanna says.

Curtis's first wife names a time and gives Joanna the address of the restaurant, but Joanna doesn't write it down. She has been there already and she knows she will have no trouble finding it again.

Chapter Ten

None of Joanna's dresses or shirts are red so, the following Monday, she drives to the department store and tries on a red sweater very much like the one the black woman wore during her own lunch with Pauline. The sweater is soft and clinging. It covers Joanna's upper arms and dips low across her chest revealing pale, smooth skin. Joanna has never seen herself dressed this way, and she studies herself for a long time in the dressing-room mirror before changing back into her own clothes. After she pays for the sweater, Joanna gets back in her car and drives home.

The following day, Joanna removes her wedding and engagement rings and places them in a drawer of her bedside table. Then she puts on the sweater and a straight black skirt and goes into the city. It is raining, not slight, indifferent rain but loud and drenching rain. Even in the short distance from her taxi to the restaurant door, Joanna is heavily spattered. Cold drops run over her shoulders and down, under the lip of the red sweater, pooling between her breasts.

The restaurant is nearly empty. Only one table is taken by a group of men who look up when she enters, their gazes firm on the glistening skin of her chest. Joanna asks for a table for two and the waiter leads her to the dark rear corner of the room. She orders a glass of wine and, when it arrives, drinks it quickly. Then she folds her hands on the tablecloth and waits.

Curtis's first wife arrives exactly on time, pausing in the vestibule to fold and fasten her dripping umbrella which she leaves in the stand just inside. She nods to the waiter and approaches Joanna smoothly, smiling as if she were greeting an old friend. 'How nice to see you,' she says happily as she sits. And then, 'You are Joanna.'

'Yes,' Joanna says.

'I'm Pauline,' Curtis's first wife says.

'Yes,' Joanna nods. 'I know.'

Pauline studies her carefully. 'You are a very beautiful woman,' she says. Joanna thanks her. The waiter comes and takes their order. Joanna asks for another glass of wine.

'Are you nervous about this meeting?' Pauline asks. Her smile is gentle, concerned.

'No,' Joanna says. 'I'm not nervous. I called you.'

'So you did,' Pauline smiles. Her curly red hair is run with grey. There are small lines around her mouth and eyes. Briefly, Joanna imagines Curtis's fingers touching this face. 'May I ask you a little about the man you mentioned before? The one who told you about us?'

'Well,' Joanna looks at her hands, still folded on the tabletop, 'I don't know much about him. I don't know his name.' Pauline watches her, silent. 'He gave me a book,' Joanna continues. 'Your telephone number was written on the title page.'

'I see,' Curtis's first wife smiles. 'Have you read this book?'

Joanna nods, her eyes on her hands.

'And what did you think of it?' Pauline says softly.

'I thought . . .' Joanna says, 'I thought I would like to work for you.'

'Good.' Pauline says simply. The waiter brings their food. Pauline eats with relish. Joanna sips her wine.

'Tell me,' Curtis's first wife says, 'how old are you Joanna?'

'Twenty eight,' Joanna says.

'And are you married?'

'No,' she says, without hesitation.

Pauline watches her carefully. 'How did you support yourself until now?'

Joanna thinks. 'I was an actress,' she says. 'I used to be an actress.'

'Good,' Pauline smiles. 'That's good. That can be helpful.' She pauses. 'Your face isn't familiar,' she says.

Joanna puts down her wine glass. 'I worked mostly in the northwest,' she says. 'In theater.' She hopes Curtis's first wife will not press farther. She has never been to the northwest.

'I see,' Pauline says. She turns to her food and eats silently. Joanna finishes her wine. Finally, Pauline sits back in the seat and turns to her.

'Let me tell you something about "O",' she says, smiling pleasantly. '"O" concerns itself primarily with issues of control. Control is our medium, our common denominator. Our clients are all men and our employees are all women, but even with that qualification there is a great deal of variety in the services we provide. No employee is forced or pressured to accept a specific assignment, or to perform any service she is uncomfortable with. An employee is free to work as much or as little as she likes, but she is required to keep and be on time for any appointment agreed to beforehand. The client pays "O" for these services, and "O" pays its employees one half of that amount. I do not cheat our employees,' Pauline says. 'No one has ever left in anger. Disillusionment, yes, but not anger.' She smiles, almost fondly, at Joanna. 'The purpose of "O" is to give pleasure,' she says. 'Sometimes we are lucky enough to give pleasure to everyone involved, employee and client alike. Do you understand what this means, Joanna?'

Joanna nods, spellbound. Pauline's hand reaches across the table and covers her own. 'Would you like to work for "O", Joanna?'

'Yes,' Joanna says.

'Yes,' Pauline echoes, her voice low. She is silent for a moment. 'I'll tell you what I would like,' she says, continuing. 'I would like to send you to see a friend of mine this afternoon for several hours. He is not a client, but you will be paid for the visit nonetheless. His name is Mr. Stephens. Are you free to see him this afternoon?'

'Yes,' Joanna nods.

'There are several reasons for this visit,' Pauline says, her voice low. 'It will help us to evaluate you, and your potential as an employee. It will give you a taste of what would be expected of you, and help you to make your own decision. You will have an opportunity to ask Mr. Stephens questions, and he will have an opportunity to give you some helpful criticism, if that is necessary. When the session is over, he and I will discuss it and I will decide whether to offer you employment with "O". Conversely, you can decide not to contact us again. If you decide not to contact us again, all three of us will forget that these meetings took place today. If you do decide to contact us, I will give you our answer then. Is this agreeable to you?'

'Yes,' Joanna says.

'Please wait here for a minute,' says Pauline. She rises and crosses the restaurant to a payphone mounted on a wall next to the kitchen. Joanna watches her dial and speak briefly. Then Pauline returns to their table and sits down.

'This is for you,' Pauline says, removing a long white envelope from her purse and handing it to Joanna. 'Here is the address,' she points to the front of the envelope. 'Inside is your payment. Please go there directly, by taxi. You are expected. Please follow Mr. Stephens' directions exactly.' Abruptly, she stands and reaches for her raincoat. Joanna stands and follows Pauline out of the restaurant. Outside, the rain has softened to a drizzle. Pauline extends her hand and Joanna takes it.

'Good luck, Joanna,' Curtis's first wife says. 'I wish you well this afternoon, and hope to speak to you again.'

'Thank you,' Joanna says.

Pauline sees a taxi over Joanna's shoulder and raises her hand to hail it. It pulls up to the curb.

'Thank you,' Joanna says again as she climbs in.

Pauline smiles, bending down. 'Enjoy yourself,' she says before turning away.

Joanna reads the address from the envelope aloud to the cab driver. He heads downtown. Slowly, she tears open the white paper. Inside are five crisp one hundred dollar bills.

Chapter Eleven

Joanna pays the driver and gets out of the taxi. The address is a tall white townhouse with elaborate iron railings over the first story windows. She climbs marble steps to the front door and pushes a thick black button. Inside, a low bell sounds.

Almost immediately, the door is opened by a tall, thickset man. He is entirely bald but the skin of his scalp is smooth and curiously compelling. He motions Joanna inside and closes the door after her.

'My name is . . .' she begins to say but he cuts her off with a swift wave of his hand.

'Don't tell me your name,' he says. His voice is deep and fierce. 'Your name is unimportant. Only my name is important, and you already know my name. That is Jeremy,' Mr. Stephens says. Joanna looks where he is pointing. Across the marble floor, a young Indonesian man waits at the foot of the stairs, his arms obediently limp at his narrow hips. 'You will go with Jeremy,' Mr. Stephens is saying. 'Jeremy will wash you. You will do precisely as Jeremy tells you to do. When Jeremy has finished with you, we will talk again. Do you agree?'

'I agree,' Joanna says. He is wonderful, Joanna thinks suddenly. She has a fleeting urge to touch the contour of his sleek head.

'Then go,' Mr. Stephens says. 'Don't wait to be told twice.'

Joanna turns and walks across the polished floor. As she nears him, Jeremy begins to climb the stairs and Joanna follows several steps back. Behind her, footsteps sound and diminish.

Jeremy climbs two flights of stairs and turns along a corridor. He opens a mahogany door and holds it for Joanna, then locks it behind her and flicks on an overhead light.

They are in a black marble bathroom, mirrored on all sides, including the ceiling. At the center of the rectangular room is a low wall of marble, about a foot high, circular, with a drain in its center. Above it a shower head protrudes from the mirror. It is, Joanna realizes, a shower without a shower curtain, like at the beach, to wash off at the end of the day. Below the shower head, a thick iron bar hangs down, horizontal. Joanna wonders what it can be for, since it looks to be directly in the downward path of the water. There is no sink, no toilet, no bidet. There is just shower, mirror, iron bar.

'Remove your clothing,' Jeremey says. His voice is thick, mottled. An accent, Joanna thinks, but there is something else.

'Everything?' she asks, but he only looks blankly at her, and she knows that he is deaf.

'Remove your clothing,' he says again, motioning with his hand for her to hurry. She steps out of her shoes and starts to unzip her skirt. Behind

Jeremy's back, the wall of mirror gives a flicker. Joanna senses the glare of eyes behind it.

She pulls off the red sweater and reaches back to unhook her bra, then hooks her thumbs inside her underwear and pulls it down. Jeremy watches, expressionless. When she is finished, he stoops and gathers her clothing and places it inside a cabinet, hidden in the marble. From the same cabinet he removes something curious and small and black, some kind of manacle, Joanna thinks. Jeremy returns to her. The manacles are rubber, and he fastens them, careful not to close them too tightly about her wrists. Then he motions with his hand for her to step backward and, when she does, he lifts the manacle overhead, fastening it to the iron bar with a buckle. Her hands are not uncomfortably bound. She moves them and grasps the metal. This is what it is for, Joanna thinks, almost happily.

Jeremy dims the light from a switch on the wall. He turns another switch and the shower over Joanna's head comes to life, first cool and weak then growing warmer and stronger. Joanna tries not to flinch. Through the wall of water, she watches the mirror, trying to meet the gaze hidden behind it.

The water stops. Jeremy holds a large tube of clear liquid and is squeezing it, letting it ooze over her skin: shoulders and chest and stomach and pubic hair. He puts the tube down and turns back again, his eyes lingering briefly at her breasts. Then his small brown hands begin to touch her, small circles at her neck and over her breasts where his thumbs brush the nipples firmly, as if they are especially dirty. Joanna bites her tongue to keep from moaning. The hands lift each breast and rub carefully in a polishing motion, gliding over the skin, then descend her ribs and abdomen. She feels a sinking, a heat between her legs. He kneels on the short marble wall and begins to wash her legs, first one then the other, squeezing them between his hands and running them up and down. Then, standing again, he reaches between them. The motion of his hand is like a beckoning, as if he were saying 'come here'. Jeremy's expression is blank, professional. He gathers fists of soapy hair.

His fingers do not enter her, and she wishes they would.

Abruptly, he straightens up and steps back. 'Turn around,' Jeremy says, circling with his hand. Joanna turns and the iron bar over her head turns with her. He coats her back with liquid from the tube and begins to spread it with his hands, running his thumbs firmly up and down her spine. Hands rub her underarms and neck. Jeremy unloosens her hair and caresses that, too, with soap, massaging her scalp. Then he reaches lower and squeezes the liquid directly into the crack of her buttocks, spreading it back and forth with the side of his thin hand. Joanna shivers, arching back to him, but he does not seem to notice.

He starts the shower again and Joanna closes her eyes, feeling the soap run down through her hair and over her body. Behind her, Jeremy is silent. After a few minutes, the water stops and he turns her again with his hands on her hips. He is holding a long black towel, and now he begins to dry her in small pats along her limbs, briefly lifting and pressing each breast, reaching back to unfold the towel along the length of her back. He dries carefully between her legs, rubbing the pubic hair, then kneels to press the towel around each thigh and calf. Finally, he motions for her to bow her head, and pulls forward her wet hair. She hears a whir as he turns on an electric dryer.

When he has finished with her, Joanna's hands are unhooked from the overhead pipe and fastened again, behind her. She leans slightly against Jeremy as he lifts first one leg then the other to roll on black stockings which end mid-thigh. He hooks them to a garter belt and fastens that too, then steps behind to fit her with a black bra, strapless, which barely covers Joanna's nipples. A pair of black high-heeled shoes are placed before her, and she steps into them. Finally, Jeremy wraps her in a large dressing gown, black silk, which, curiously, has no arms. He ties the silk belt at her waist.

There is a tap at the mirrored wall. Jeremy motions for her to follow, and opens the door. Joanna walks behind him down the carpeted hall. Her wrists rub behind her back, slightly uncomfortable. At the end of the hall, Jeremy opens a black door and waits for her to pass through it. The room is large and dim. Joanna can discern an array of objects, tables, chairs, couches, and some things which defy classification made of wood and straps with metallic buckles. 'Walk to the center of the room and face me,' Mr. Stephens' voice says. She turns her head. He is sitting, cross-legged, in a black armchair. Joanna sees the glow of his cigarette, the rising coil of smoke. She walks farther into the room and stops a few feet from him. Behind her, the door shuts with a heavy click. A minute later, Jeremy's hands fumble at her waist, untying the robe. It slips off easily and he takes it away and goes to stand behind the armchair.

For a long moment, nothing is said. They merely watch her and Joanna watches them doing it. Jeremy's expression is blank, but Mr. Stephens examines her with frank interest, scrutinizing her breasts and crotch. His scalp shines in the dim light. Joanna presses her thighs together and feels moisture. Her nipples harden inside the bra.

'You are here for evaluation,' he says suddenly, without preamble. 'You are here at our request, but at your own consent. Your silence implies consent.' He pauses. Joanna watches the smoke of his cigarette. 'You may leave at any time,' Mr. Stephens continues, 'simply by asking to leave. If you ask to leave, we will immediately stop whatever we are doing. You will be given your clothing and allowed to go. We will not ask you to return the money we have given you. If you leave at your own request you will forget completely about this meeting. You will make no attempt to contact either myself or "O" ever again, and we will make no attempt to locate and contact you. Do you understand?'

Joanna nods.

'Answer aloud,' Mr. Stephens says.

'I understand,' says Joanna. Her voice is flat, expressionless.

'You should be aware that every aspect of this session will be discussed with "O" in detail. How you look, feel, smell and taste. There will be no privacy. Do you understand?'

'Yes,' Joanna says.

'You will be penetrated vaginally, orally and anally. Do you understand?'

'Yes,' Joanna says.

'You may experience some discomfort. You may also experience some pain. At "O" we do not advocate the causing of gratuitous pain. We believe in causing pain to the point of pleasure. Clients of "O" are forbidden brutality of any kind, but many enjoy experimentation. Do you understand?'

'Yes,' Joanna says.

'At the end of this session, you will have an opportunity to ask questions. Until then, you are not to speak unless directly asked a question, or, naturally, unless you have decided to leave. Do you understand?'

'Yes,' Joanna says.

'Pauline tells me that you have experience as an actress. You may find it helpful. Often, you will have to decide for yourself what attitude . . . what character is desired of you. For the purposes of this session, I would like you to pretend that you are here unwillingly. You are neither defiant nor submissive. You are afraid that you will be hurt if you do not comply with my wishes. Do you understand?'

'Yes,' Joanna says.

Mr. Stephens puts out his cigarette and rises slowly. He is wearing a black silk robe like the one Joanna wore, but with arms. He walks towards her and stops less than a foot away. In her high-heels Joanna is nearly his height and their faces are very close. Involuntarily, she begins to tremble. Mr. Stephens watches her carefully.

Suddenly, she feels his hands at the sides of her breasts. He pulls roughly at the strapless bra, yanking it down until it rests over her garter belt. Her nipples are hard and throbbing. With his thumb and forefinger, he pinches the right one and twists, like a switch. Joanna's eyes widen but she says nothing. He twists the other one with his left hand, then both together, slowly, back and forth. Joanna moans, her eyes on his face. 'Shut up,' Mr. Stephens says, simply.

His hands grab at her breasts, caressing them roughly. His thumbs meet between them. Abruptly, he bends down and takes a nipple in his mouth. Joanna feels his lips, his tongue, then the crush of his teeth around it. His hand on the other breast is still. She is breathing quickly. She would like to touch his smooth head, holding him against her, but her wrists twist in their rubber manacle behind her back. His teeth gnaw at her nipple, then his lips cover it and he sucks loudly, making sounds, then he torments her again with his teeth. Her cunt aches and seeps.

He straightens up and puts his hands on her shoulders. His lips are red and glistening. He presses her down. 'Kneel,' Mr. Stephens says. There is urgency in the word, Joanna thinks, but his face is calm. She is awkward on her heels but the hands on her shoulders steady her. She kneels at his feet and his hands calmly undo the belt of his robe, parting it. He is naked underneath, pale and nearly hairless. His cock is short and thick. It tilts against one thigh, throbbing slightly. His fingers lock behind her head and he presses into her face, rubbing himself over her nose and mouth. She catches the scent of him, ammonia and almonds. A drop of salt is dragged over her lips. She keeps her mouth closed tightly and tries to pull away but he holds her head firm. His own hand reaches for his cock and lifts it, its head at her lips. He brushes it back and forth.

'Open your mouth,' he says. Joanna's lips part but her jaw remains locked. He waits a moment, then slips a thumb into the corner of her mouth, behind her teeth, then pries her open like a horse forced to accept a bridle. 'Don't disobey,' he says softly. And then: 'You will have to be punished.'

One hand twists her hair. The other guides his cock into Joanna's mouth. His pubic hair bristles in her nostrils. His hips circle and begin to thrust. His cock fills her cheeks and flattens her tongue. She gasps through her nose. He finds the back of her throat and hits it over and over. 'Suck me,' he hisses, and she does, gulping at him, sliding from foot to tip. He seems to thicken between her lips. He rocks into her. She hears his low wail and swallows that too. Her wrists chafe against each other. She wants to grab him. He starts to come, a warm leak then a punch at the ridged roof of her mouth. He thrusts deep and hard. She is aware of his knees, pressing her shoulders between them, the yanks in her hair, the thick salt coursing down her throat. Suddenly he pulls back. She knows he hasn't finished. Standing over her, he yanks at her hair until her head tilts back, then shoots semen over her face, hot and sticky and white.

When Joanna opens her eyes, Mr. Stephens has not moved. His cock is limp in his hand, and flushed red. He is watching her face, which stings with drying semen. 'Get up,' he says finally. She climbs unsteadily to her feet.

Turning her roughly, he nudges her ahead of him across the room to a strange leather chair with steel arm and footrests. Mr. Stephens unfastens her wrists and brings them to her sides. 'Sit,' he says.

The chair is cool and smooth and tilts slightly back. Mr. Stephens fastens her arms to the armrests with buckled leather straps. Other straps fasten her feet, each to its own footrest. The leather panel beneath her thighs suddenly folds down, leaving only a ledge to perch on. He presses a button on the side of the chair and slowly the footrests begin to move apart, spreading her wider and wider. She tries to keep her knees together but the chair is insistent, irrefutable. She is stretched and separated, her knees bent, as if she were giving birth. Mr. Stephens presses the button again and the chair stops, freezing her open. He leans forward and fastens a final strap, this one at the underside of her breasts, pushing them slightly up.

Turning, Mr. Stephens motions to Jeremy who responds immediately, walking swiftly to the chair and carrying a low footstool and something else, a light, Joanna realizes. Mr. Stephens takes the footstool and settles it on the floor between Joanna's outstretched legs, and sits. Jeremy switches on the light which is strong and bright. Standing behind Mr. Stephens, he points it over his head at Joanna's crotch. Joanna shudders. She has never felt so open, so exposed. Mr. Stephens, his gaze firm on her cunt, does not look up.

Delicately, his fingers unhook the garter straps behind and in front of her thighs, and roll the stockings to just above Joanna's knees. He combs the pubic hair which covers her cunt and carefully lifts it, parting it, moving it aside. She feels the back of his hands against her inner thighs, testing the softness of her skin. He rubs his cheeks against them, first one then the other, almost thoughtfully. Then, sitting back slightly he begins to explore her, touching and tracing the thick outer lips, prickly with hair, then the smooth, slicked inner lips. His touch is questioning, curious, almost clinical, but Joanna cannot stop herself from moaning with pleasure.

Immediately he looks up, his face contorted, outraged. 'I told you to shut up,' he shouts. Jerking to his feet, he reaches down to deliver a stinging slap to the tender skin of her thigh, then the other side. Jeremy, standing behind him, does not move.

Mr. Stephens turns and walks briskly across the room and out the door, tying his silk robe as he goes. Jeremy stands motionless, training the light on her crotch. She can't see his face behind it. Her heart beats wildly. When she attempts to move, the strap at her breasts cuts into them. She tries to relax.

After a minute he returns, still fierce, carrying two pieces of black fabric. 'When you learn to obey, it will not be necessary to gag you,' he says, matter of factly, forcing one piece into her mouth and tying it behind her head. The other scarf covers her eyes. Through it, she can only faintly still see the light.

There is a rush of warmth between her thighs. Mr. Stephens has returned to his seat, and the fingers begin again, slowly, lingering, as if daring her to moan again and invite more punishment. She feels the warmth of his breath, and knows that he is close, inspecting, perhaps smelling her. Up and down the fingers travel, moving every fold of skin to search behind it. Her pubic hair is pulled gently, then harder. The heat is intense. Finally, a finger pauses at the opening of her cunt and circles wetly at the rim. She feels open, slicked with need, focused on the length of it. It enters slowly, joint by joint, sinking in and then moving in a stroking motion. She resists the urge to grab at it with her own muscles. The finger withdraws and two fingers take its place and continue stroking. When they slip out, she feels his two hands snaking round her thighs to the front, then carefully separating the lips of her cunt, holding them apart. His tongue glides into her, thick and pulsing. Joanna feels herself melt around it. His face pushes against her, rubbing from side to side as the tongue flicks and laps, tasting her. She imagines his cheeks wet with her and the thought makes her bite down on the fabric, straining against her own pleasure.

He makes no sound of his own. The tongue slips out and begins to lick the insides of her thighs, releasing the lingering sting of his slaps. She feels his mouth at the edges of her cunt, nibbling, taking gentle bites, then the broad flat of his tongue again in a lapping motion, up and up and up until his lips settle just below the rim of her pubic bone and begin to suck.

Joanna strains against her straps but she can barely move. She knows that he is testing her, waiting to see how much she can take. She also knows that he sucks her not for her pleasure but out of narrow curiosity: how hard is it, will it move beneath his tongue, what will it taste like? She grits her teeth, determined, but the motion of his tongue, the slight sucking sounds she can just make out are unbearable. Involuntarily, she arches against him, making what movement she is free to make and pressing further into his mouth, wanting to explode down his throat just as he did down hers.

But as soon as she does, it is over. The lips freeze and then part and draw away. She hears him settle back on his stool. He is watching, she thinks, panting. Her breasts rise into the leather strap. An eternity passes. Slowly, she feels the urgency leave her.

A hand returns to her cunt and fingers stretch the opening. Something cool and stiff is pressed against her, rubbed clinically for lubrication then pushed inside. Joanna knows, instinctively, that Mr. Stephens has not moved. The thing inside her is harder than flesh. It probes her and then, slowly, is removed. Almost immediately, another object enters her, larger and longer. It, too, probes and is taken away. Rubber, Joanna thinks. He is testing my size.

Five phalluses in all are pushed into her cunt, carefully but firmly. They grow larger and thicker and she feels stretched and pulled. The last one refuses to travel farther than a few inches. She imagines it protruding from her. Gently, his fingers ease it out and take it away.

A minute later, those fingers are at her ankles, unbuckling. Hands brush her breasts, removing the strap beneath them, then travel to her arms. She feels them come free.

'Get up,' Mr. Stephens says. Slowly, Joanna brings her knees together. The joints ache. She sits up and finds the floor with her high heels. Holding onto the chair behind her, she gets to her feet. 'Jeremy will lead you,' Mr. Stephens says from across the room. His voice is brisk, businesslike. A slim hand settles on Joanna's wrist. She steps blindly, shakily, following him.

When he stops, she stands, quivering in the darkness. She senses the nearness of another object, the closeness of Mr. Stephens' breath. 'You will take a step up on your knees, then bend forward,' the voice says. 'Feel with your knees.' Joanna does. There is a ledge, like a high step, covered with something rubbery and soft. She climbs onto it, rests for a moment on her knees, then begins to bend. Abruptly, a hand grabs her head and forces it forward more roughly, pressing her face against a leather surface. There is a thick round cushion under her hips, raising them higher than the rest of her. She feels as if she is lying over a mound. A hand fastens a leather strap behind her back, then her wrists are bound together and attached to it. She turns her cheek to the cool leather, and sighs.

Joanna feels the silk of Mr. Stephens' gown brushing over her back. A light finger slides down the crack between her buttocks, then, abruptly, her right leg is lifted and moved. She feels a strap tighten around it, just above the knee. Next, the other knee is taken and moved and strapped. She is in a position like praying, her head down, her ass raised, her legs bent beneath her and spread. Behind the hump of the cushion at her hips, the length of her vulva is open, unfurled. She senses the nearness of his face to it. A casual fingertip touches her anus and a quiver runs through her. 'Try to relax,' he says, almost kindly. 'You will find this less painful if you are relaxed.'

His hands settle on her ass, moving the flesh, squeezing it, testing its firmness, then gliding down the backs of her thighs. The motion is both teasing and comforting. She lets herself sink into it, warm to it but then, suddenly, he stops and steps back. Automatically, Joanna tenses again. There is a whistle. Something long, slender and hard flicks through the air and lands, stinging the skin of her left buttock, then rises again and beats the right. Joanna thinks rather than feels pain, but the actual sensation is a mild, almost sweet sting. He continues to use the whip, pausing after every few strokes to caress her ass and inner thighs with his other hand. Once or twice, the whip itself is drawn lazily through the crack of her buttocks. Once or twice, its tip is brought close to her anus, where it vibrates.

He turns his attention to the backs of her thighs, striking them softly with the whip while the fingers of his other hand creep into her cunt. Ignoring his command (after all, he is already punishing her), Joanna moans. If Mr. Stephens hears, he doesn't react. Stepping behind her he kneels between her open knees. His fingers still move inside her and now he disposes of the whip and begins to slap her buttocks. She feels blood rush to them, imagines them red and furious. She wishes she could see them like this.

The fingers slip from her cunt. His other hand moves over her anus and, very gently, begins to touch it, pulling it, separating it. Joanna hears the suck of a tube being squeezed. Something cool and gelatinous is deposited in the crack of her ass. 'Try to relax,' he says. Slowly, he begins to rub, first the tops of her thighs where they meet the buttocks, then the globes of muscle, tingling from the slaps and whip, then the narrow valley from coccyx to cunt and finally the hole itself. A finger circles it, working the lubricant in. She feels him stand behind her, hears the squeeze of the tube again, this time directly against her anus. Two smaller hands slide around her hips and press the buttocks apart. Jeremy, she thinks. There is a rustle of silk, his robe undone and pulled apart, then the cool penetration of his finger, boring through the sphincter muscle and into her rectum, slipping its length into her. Joanna cries out, her gag muffling but not preventing the sound. The finger twists and tests then withdraws. Joanna exhales, relieved. But two fingers present themselves and, against her will, the sphincter opens to admit them. Stop, Joanna thinks. She almost says it aloud but then remembers what will happen if she does, and bites her tongue. Come on then, she tells herself. Let's get it over with.

The two fingers pull slowly out. Joanna hears a grunt, then, to her surprise, Mr. Stephens rises from his knees and steps around to her shoulder. Immediately, Jeremy's hands slip from her buttocks. 'I'm too thick for you,' she hears him say. 'I'm afraid we'll need another arrangement.' Without warning, he removes her gag and blindfold and she blinks at him, trying to make him out. When Joanna's eyes adjust, they focus on Mr. Stephens, the belt of his robe tied again at his hips. Jeremy stands beside him, stripped to the waist, his slim body hairless and childlike. As Joanna watches, Mr. Stephens' fingers unbutton Jeremy's fly and pull down his trousers, then roll down his underwear. Nonchalantly, Jeremy steps out of his clothes and stands naked in front of her. The expression on his face is vacant, but his cock is rock hard, veined and straining. It is narrow but excessively long. Mr. Stephens places protective hands on Jeremy's shoulders. 'I can use the rubber phalluses again,' he is saying. 'I'm sure you would prefer that. But I think Jeremy will enjoy this. Don't you?' He smiles and waits for her response. This is the moment, she is thinking, when he expects her to ask to leave. She grits her teeth, then remembers that she is supposed to be afraid.

'Please don't hurt me,' Joanna says, trying to whimper. 'Do anything you want, but please, please don't hurt me.' She turns her head away and pretends to cry. Behind her, she hears his low laugh.

Hands part her ass again, broad hands this time. There is a soft brush of skin as Jeremy climbs up behind her. She tries to breathe deeply when he splits her open, cold and wet, pushing deep into her bowels, drawing back and pushing again. Jeremy's sounds are mottled, guttural. He leans forward, grabbing the strap at her waist to pull himself farther inside. Each thrust is a sharp and radiating pain through Joanna's body. He rocks on top of her, wild, one hand absently slapping her back between the shoulderblades in time with his pounding. She hears shouts, a final rhythm of quick pounding as he comes, emptying himself deep within her. Joanna imagines she can feel the heat shooting up to her heart as he relaxes, breathing heavily against her back.

Jeremy pulls back and drops out of her. Immediately he kneels and unbuckles the straps behind her knees. At the same time, Mr. Stephens releases the buckle at her back. Her wrists come apart and are stretched over her head and refastened. 'Turn over,' he says. Joanna turns on her back, her ass resting high on the pillow, her legs hanging free. She expects her ankles to be refastened, but they are not. A rubber phallus is inserted, quickly and expertly, into her cunt. Mr. Stephens kneels between her open thighs and swiftly begins to lick her, tenderly, like an animal. Desire floods back into her crotch. Dimly, she feels the fluid seep from her anus. His mouth is passionate now, and hungry. He finds her center and sucks loudly, rhythmically. This is a reward, Joanna thinks. She rubs against him and he responds, giving her what she wants. His hand rises and motions. Instantly Jeremy falls over her and begins to feed at her breasts, urgently sucking one with his mouth, pressing and squeezing the other between his fingers. Joanna cries out loud. She moves frantically. At the verge of her climax Mr. Stephens suddenly stands and removes the rubber phallus, filling her with his own swollen cock. His thumb rubs where his mouth had been a moment before, smoothly but with friction.

ELIZABETH BENNETT

Her nipples throb in Jeremy's mouth and fingers. Joanna arches and writhes, her ankles locked around Mr. Stephens' waist. When she opens her eyes, she sees him grinning, waiting for her, and she comes and comes and comes.

Chapter Twelve

Afterwards, Jeremy takes her back to the bathroom and washes her again. Her hands are free, but Joanna is not permitted to touch herself. She stands limply as he rubs soap over her breasts and between her legs, attentively but as if he has no particular familiarity with these places. This time, he rinses her with a hand-held shower, motions for her to bend forward and lets the generous stream of water run into her cunt and anus. He leaves her to dry herself, then brings her clothes and stands blankly, watching her change into them. When Joanna is ready, he takes her downstairs to the study next to the front door.

Mr. Stephens, dressed in casual pants and a clean, pressed shirt, is seated behind a heavy desk. He motions for her to take a seat and she does, demurely crossing her legs. Mr. Stephens lights a cigarette. 'You did well,' he says flatly. 'Frankly, I was surprised. You were a little defiant at first in the bathroom, looking for me behind the mirror. I thought you would ask to leave.' Joanna is silent. 'Do you have any questions?'

'Will there always be whips?' Asks Joanna.

'No. Few of our clients enjoy using whips, though many like to administer spankings, or some other light manual punishment. The "No Brutality" restriction means that whips can only be used lightly, for effect. As I used it,' he adds, after a pause. 'You didn't mind it, I saw.'

'No,' Joanna says. She is silent for a moment. Finally she says, 'I didn't like being fucked in the ass.'

'Ah,' says Mr. Stephens. 'We will have to bear that in mind. To some extent, "O" can take care of the problem, simply by not sending you to clients who enjoy anal sex. Conversely, though, you may find that you grow to like it.'

'Possibly,' Joanna says. She is doubtful.

'You are a beautiful woman,' Mr. Stephens says. 'I have enjoyed our session.' He pauses. 'I also enjoyed watching you come, but I must warn you that not all of our clients will want you to come. You are aware of that?'

'Yes,' Joanna says.

He gets to his feet and, rather formally, extends his hand. 'Thank you for visiting with me,' Mr. Stephens says. 'I will speak with Pauline this evening. I hope she will hear from you soon.'

'Thank you,' Joanna says. She turns and leaves the study. Jeremy is standing calmly by the front door, waiting to let her out. His face contains no message of its own. When she steps out onto the street, Joanna's heart begins to beat loudly. The air is soft and moist and heavy, the passersby are self-contained and busy, and everything seems relentlessly normal.

Chapter Thirteen

'This is Joanna,' she says the following morning when Pauline answers the phone.

'Joanna!' The voice is warm, delighted. 'I'm so pleased to hear from you. Mr. Stephens was very impressed with you.'

'Thank you,' Joanna says.

'And you have had a chance to think about us?'

'Yes,' says Joanna.

'And you are still interested in working for "O".'

'Yes,' Joanna says. 'Yes, I am.'

'Good.' Pauline pauses briefly. 'Then we would like to offer you a job.'

'I'm free to work in the afternoons,' says Joanna, grateful for the first time since her marriage that she is a woman of leisure.

PART TWO

'O'

Chapter Fourteen

Joanna's first assignment for 'O' is to meet a woman named Clarissa in an apartment downtown, for a party.

'What kind of a party?' Joanna asks Pauline over the phone.

'For clients,' Pauline explains. 'Clarissa will tell you what to do.'

Joanna asks what she should wear, thinking briefly of the conservative dresses she occasionally wears to dinner or parties with Curtis's friends, but Pauline informs her that Clarissa will take care of that. 'She's an old hand at this,' Pauline laughs. 'Just do as she tells you and you'll be fine.'

On the day of the party, Joanna takes the train to the city. The address she has been given is near the financial district, a low brick building nestled behind a street of depressed-looking shop fronts. There is no downstairs bell, so Joanna climbs to the top floor and knocks.

Clarissa opens the door, dressed in a hastily tied terrycloth robe, wet from the bath. 'Come in, Joanna,' she says in a high singsong voice. 'You caught me just as I was getting out.' Joanna steps inside.

Clarissa is short but voluptuous, with flaming red hair hanging damply to her shoulders. 'Come with me while I finish getting ready,' she beckons, turning back down the hall. 'Then we'll start on you.'

Joanna follows her to the back of the apartment. There are no visible windows, and the overhead lighting is dim. They pass first through a large, comfortable living room, strewn with chairs. In the fireplace, a small gas fire dances and snaps. 'Is this where the party will be?' Joanna asks, and Clarissa nods, yes.

'And back there,' she points, indicating a closed door. 'I'll show you around before they arrive.'

In the bathroom, Clarissa pulls the plug in the bathtub, and water begins to drain. 'Do you want a bath?' She asks.

'No,' Joanna says, noticing a bidet in the corner. 'I think I'll just wash a bit. Pauline said you'd have something for me to wear.'

'Yeah,' Clarissa says, laughing. 'But I doubt you'll be wearing it for long.' She turns and looks intently at Joanna. 'This is your first thing for "O", isn't it?'

'Yes,' Joanna says.

Clarissa smiles. 'Don't be nervous,' she says. 'I get to do most of the work here. You'll probably end up mostly watching.'

'Okay,' Joanna says, feeling nervous anyway.

While Joanna washes at the bidet, Clarissa slips out of her robe and begins to dry herself off with a towel. 'Excuse me a minute,' she says, turning on an electric dryer. She bends slightly forward to rub her wet hair under it and Joanna notices, for the first time, the pale skin of Clarissa's ass. It is puckered with welts, thin red lines of healing cuts, the shadows of old bruises. Involuntarily, she shudders, unable to take her eyes from them. She stands and dries her crotch with a towel, then takes off the rest of her clothes and sits on the toilet to wait.

Clarissa takes a small pot of red lip gloss and darkens her lips, and then her nipples. 'You too,' she says, passing it to Joanna and watching intently as she does the same. She unpins Joanna's hair and smooths it up and back, over her head. 'Pretty,' Clarissa smiles. 'You have great hair.'

'Thanks,' Joanna mumbles.

'This is what you wear,' she says, holding up a piece of black lace with stiff cupping at one end and no discernible zipper. 'I'll show you how to get it on, it's a bit confusing.' She helps Joanna step into it, pulling it carefully up her torso until the stiff end comes to rest beneath Joanna's breasts. They aren't cups, she now sees. Instead, a stiff ridge supports her breasts from beneath, pushing them up but not covering the nipples. Clarissa, appraising her, frowns and administers more lip gloss to the tips and Joanna shudders slightly at the brush of her fingers. She has never been touched this way by a woman.

Beneath her breasts, the black lace hugs her torso, letting much of her skin show through. At Joanna's hips, the fabric expands slightly in a kind of skirt, covering her buttocks and descending a few inches down her thighs, barely hiding her crotch. 'What do I wear underneath?' Joanna asks, but Clarissa only smiles.

She puts on boots, black leather, which lace up to her ankles and have high, spiky heels. Joanna, wobbly at first, takes a few steps around the bathroom to steady herself. Clarissa changes into a white silk slip, tight across her large breasts. Joanna watches as she steps into white underpants, also silk, and gently eases it over her scarred and bruised ass. Clarissa remains barefoot, but before she leaves the bathroom she fastens a thin black band, made of some unidentifiable metal, to her wrist. Then, to Joanna's surprise, Clarissa hands her an identical band and tells her to put it on. 'You'll keep this,' Clarissa says. 'Wear it whenever you're going to meet a client. It's a way for him to recognize you.'

Joanna puts it on and admires it. The metal is cool against her skin, and shiny. 'Let's go,' Clarissa says.

They walk back through the apartment to the large living room. Clarissa lights tall candles in brass candle holders scattered around the room and they flicker warmly, picking up the glow of the small fire. At a bar in the corner, she takes out crystal glasses and places them on a silver tray, nine glasses.

'Nine clients will be coming,' Clarissa says, opening a bottle of scotch and pouring generously into each glass, then adding ice. 'You stand at the door and give them their drinks. They know where to put their coats, and whatever else they bring, so you don't have to worry about that. Don't talk unless you're spoken to, don't look anyone in the eye. When all nine are here, lock the front door and come into the living room. If anyone needs more to drink, it's here,' she says, indicating the bar.

'Where will you be?' Joanna asks.

'Come,' Clarissa says. She has finished with the tray and now beckons for Joanna to follow. 'In here,' she says, opening the door she had indicated earlier.

They pass through it into a small room. Clarissa lights candles here too, and Joanna can see that the walls are bare, stone colored. A series of chains hang from them in pairs, dangling manacles. In the center of the room there is a low platform, covered with some leathery materials, black and shiny. At each corner of the platform, a wooden post rises, each with its own manacled chain attached. Looking at it, Joanna's heart begins to pound longingly. She suspects that Clarissa will be the one to be stretched here, and she wishes it were her instead.

'You'll have to fasten me,' Clarissa is saying. She walks quickly around the room, plumping the chairs and couches which line three of the walls. A table is pushed against the fourth wall, near the dangled chains, and here she pauses, picking up a roll of black tape from an array of objects: whips and phalluses and fat tubes of lubricant. 'Any more questions?' She smiles, ripping off a short section. 'Speak now or forever hold your peace.'

Joanna swallows, watching her. 'Clarissa,' she says, 'Do you enjoy being whipped?'

Clarissa looks at Joanna for a long moment before she speaks. 'Yes,' she says finally, expressionless.

She walks to the wall and faces it, expectantly. Joanna lifts her wrists and fastens them into the manacles. Clarissa's feet are then fastened to chains on the floor, a short distance out into the room so that she is spread slightly, and forced to lean against the wall. 'The tape,' she says calmly, and Joanna fastens it across her mouth. As she does, they both hear the first knock at the door.

'You okay?' Joanna whispers. Clarissa nods. 'Okay then,' she says, backing away. 'See you in a bit.' She turns and leaves the room, closing its door behind her, then takes her tray to the entryway.

Two men brush past her when she lets them in, taking two of the glasses from her tray, shrugging off their jackets. She hears a rustle as they are hung up, a closet door closing. They go into the living room and talk quietly. Another knock and three men enter. Her tray lightens in her hands as more glasses are taken. Joanna looks at the floor. She is aware of eyes, studying her body through the lace, lingering over her pushed-up breasts and darkened nipples, but no one speaks to her. From the living room she begins to hear laughter, as from old and intimate friends meeting. A man arrives alone. Joanna steals a glance at him as he passes her without comment: tall, bull-necked and broad. She senses cruelty in him, even from behind, and shudders. Finally, the last three enter, all together, and take the remaining glasses from her tray. She locks the door behind them and goes into the living room, her eyes on her own feet.

Low voices and sporadic laughter. Just like any other cocktail party, Joanna thinks, smiling to herself. An empty glass is presented to her and Joanna pours scotch into it, adding ice. As she does, a hand reaches to touch her breast, lightly, near the nipple. Involuntarily, Joanna looks up, meeting the eyes of the man, and instantly he slaps her, stinging her cheek. She gasps and looks down again. Across the room someone says, solemnly, 'She's new. She'll need to be taught.' Joanna feels a room full of eyes on her and breathes heavily, the leather stiff against her breasts.

Suddenly, the crack of a whip shatters the silence, then a moan. Clarissa, she thinks. There is a collective shuffle in the living room. Someone takes Joanna's hand. 'Come with me,' a voice says, kind and vaguely elderly. It pulls her gently and she follows. 'Come,' it says again. 'We'll watch together.'

She lets herself be led into the adjoining room, sensing the bodies of the men before her and behind her, then, gently, she is pulled down onto the lap of the man whose hand she holds. They are in a deep chair, plush but armless. Beneath her, she feels him, stiff inside his pants, probing her through the fabric. His hands fold across her waist. 'Look,' he tells her, speaking into Joanna's ear. 'It's all right to look.'

Joanna looks up. The bull-necked man she noticed earlier stands by the far wall, examining the objects on the table top. One by one, he lifts the whips, running his fingers along their lengths, bending them between his hands until they crackle. The other men, settled on couches and chairs around the room watch silently, sipping their drinks. Clarissa, still clothed in her slip and underpants, is motionless, manacled to the wall, her head hung down, but each time a whip is cracked through the air she moans and cringes.

Finally, the man makes his selection, a slender riding crop, black, with no tassel. Turning to Clarissa, he takes a fist of her hair and raises her head, gliding the crop over her cheeks and throat. She moans in terror. Briefly, Joanna feels the lap beneath her shift, a low groan at her ear.

A hand runs down Clarissa's back, then reaches around her to feel her breasts and belly. Her legs are stiff, slightly apart, the calf muscles bulging. Carefully, her crotch is felt, in front and behind, then slowly the whip is inched beneath the white silk slip, and lifted over her buttocks. He pushes it up her back and rolls it in front of her shoulders, letting the whip brush her shoulderblades, then he steps back.

The first blow lands on the backs of Clarissa's thighs and is followed, immediately, by the man's other hand, tracing the sudden welts. Clarissa jerks from his touch and the whip descends again, punishing her this time, cracking against her flesh. The stiff length of leather is drawn lazily across her lower back and over her ass, then slowly between her legs. Clarissa writhes, moaning, and is punished again. 'Hold still,' the man growls, speaking for the first time. 'If you move again I'll whip your cunt.'

Joanna's breath catches. Clarissa freezes, the muscles of her buttocks visibly tightening. The man leans his whip against the wall, where she can see it, and steps behind her. Kneeling between her legs, he slowly pulls at the white silk of her underwear, drawing it back across the marred skin of Clarissa's ass. An admiring finger is drawn over the scars. There is a murmur of approval from the watching men. He peels down the silk until it rests beneath her buttocks, held in place by its elastic, then stands and steps to her side again. 'Nice,' someone comments.

The bull-necked man takes up his whip again, cracking it lightly against his own leg. The fingers of his left hand brush Clarissa's buttocks, patting them. Then, abruptly, he spreads her ass and probes stiffly against her anus, snorting with distaste. 'Tight,' Joanna hears him mutter. 'We'll have to fix that, won't we?'

He takes a tube of lubricant from the table and smears it thickly along the length of the leather crop, then slowly draws through the crack of her ass. A finger follows in its wake, also lubricated, and rubs the hole, forcing it open. Clarissa groans deeply, her head down. The finger twists and presses and finally sinks, disappearing into her body.

Joanna, remembering her own experience with Mr. Stephens, pities her.

When he finally withdraws, the man begins to whip her again, this time with a longer, more slender switch. Clarissa's buttocks jerk slightly as each stroke makes contact, snapping against her flesh. She screams into the tape over her mouth, but the sound only seems to drive the man further into a frenzy. He roughly fingers her inner thighs, grabbing between to feel her cunt through the bunched silk of her underpants. Then, leaning forward, he suddenly licks Clarissa's ass until it glistens, highlighting the fresh welts he has given her.

'Let's take her down,' someone says. The bull-necked man puts down his whip and unfastens her wrists. Clarissa leans heavily against the wall as her ankles are released, then she is harshly turned to face the room. For a long moment she stands, limply, in front of her tormentor. The white slip flutters to her hips. Then he reaches in front of her and takes her breasts in his hands, pushing them together. Clarissa's eyes widen and she looks fearfully around the room, taking in the watching men but avoiding Joanna's gaze. It is a long moment, tensely silent. Then the man behind her grasps Clarissa's slip in both hands and tears, pulling the fabric apart, releasing her large breasts. Several men get up from their seats and take hold of her, grabbing her limbs, pulling and lifting her towards the low platform. Clarissa struggles wildly, her shrieks muffled by the tape, but they are too many and too strong. They push her down and spread her open, snapping the manacles about her wrists and feet. The slip is ripped again and it comes apart. Someone pulls it from beneath her and throws it aside. Her underpants are yanked to mid-thigh then cut away with a pair of scissors, and she is naked, her breasts heaving. A pair of hands lifts Clarissa's ass and a pillow is slid beneath it, raising her open cunt until it is almost at Joanna's eye level.

The men sitting at the edges of the platform look down with interest at the body between them and begin to touch it, lifting Clarissa's breasts and pinching her darkened nipples, stroking her inner thighs. She writhes beneath their hands, twisting away from them, but they take little notice. The bull-necked man thoughtfully fingers the thick patch of red hair at her crotch, twisting and pulling. 'She will need to be shaved,' he says finally, almost wistfully, Joanna thinks, as if it is a bother.

A razor is brought, and lubricant spread between Clarissa's legs. Carefully, intently, they begin to shave her, the four heads close together over her crotch. Joanna hears her whimper, her head rolling back and forth at the top of the platform, eyes tight. After every few strokes of the razor, hair is wiped away with a cloth, then the razor continues until they are finally spreading her thighs to shave their inner edges, along the cunt, wiping her clean. When they are finished with her she is almost childlike, Joanna thinks, her heavy breasts a poignant contrast to the bare innocence between her legs.

The men fall on her, covering her with their hands. One begins to spread oil over her belly and over her chest, then another takes the oil and spreads it farther down, slicking her legs with it.

Another man rubs her arms and underarms, and reaches beneath her to coat Clarissa's back. Joanna seeps with envy, imagining so many hands on her own body, owning it and feeling it. She stares at the platform, entranced. Slowly, she becomes aware of another hand, reaching forward from behind her chair, softly stroking her breast.

The bull-necked man kneels at Clarissa's head, his crotch over her face. As she stares up at him, he slowly unzips himself and eases down his own trousers, taking his pulsing cock in his hand. He lowers himself then, straddling her face and rubbing against it, rolling his cock over her nose and cheeks. He reaches forward to pinch Clarissa's breasts, then surrenders them to the hands and mouths of the other men. The man rises again to his knees and stares between them, then, almost tenderly, unpeels the heavy tape over Clarissa's mouth. She gasps when it comes away. He reaches beneath her neck to lift it, her head tilting back, mouth open, then smoothly enters her. Joanna hears the rasp of breath at her own ear. Then her other breast is taken and rubbed, the fingers rough at her nipple, and she moans loudly.

Hands massage Clarissa's cunt, penetrating her deeply. One man lowers himself and begins to lick her, briefly, then gets to his knees and strips and thrusts into her only a few times before he comes, groaning. Someone else pulls him away and takes his place, then another. The man at her head continues fucking her mouth, moaning, lost in himself. Something is lifting Joanna, hands beneath her arms, bringing her to her feet then turning her and pushing her down again, bent over the lap she has been sitting on. Hands lift the short skirt and push it forward. Her ass is smacked by a flat palm, then lovingly stroked, then smacked again. A finger enters her and she moans, writhing. Behind her, Joanna's legs are forced apart. A body lowers itself between them.

She gasps when the tongue glides into her, pushing back against it, and then she is punished for that by the tongue's withdrawal. Hands slap her thighs, separating them further. A lap appears beneath her head, inches from her face. She watches a zipper sliding down, a throbbing cock emerging from it, then is told to lick and she does lick, wanting to swallow it whole. Behind her, a thrust and she is entered, deeply, and pounded. Hands cup her breasts. She feels the clamp of wrists at her ankles, holding them firmly, far apart. The cock in Joanna's mouth finds the back of her throat and explodes, stinging wetly down her throat. She is surrounded by moans, behind her, above her, across the room where the men take their turns with Clarissa, then the violent, growling climax which can only come from the bull-necked man, and finally her own, obliterating everything else with its suddenness and force, sharp and stunning and unexpected as a slender finger slips into her rectum, and beckons.

Chapter Fifteen

'Welcome to "O",' Clarissa says dreamily in her bath. Her hands are folded behind her, supporting her head. Joanna, who has already bathed, sits wrapped in a robe on the toilet. All of the men are gone.

'Are you okay?' Joanna asks.

'Mm, good,' says Clarissa. 'I came twice. Once at the wall and again, near the end. You?'

'Yes,' Joanna says, feeling herself blush.

Clarissa sighs, happily. 'I love that man,' she says. 'He knows all about me.'

Joanna begins to pin up her hair. 'Do you know anything much about him?'

'Not much,' Clarissa says, sitting up in the bath and pulling the plug. 'He works with money, I know that. Joanna,' she laughs, shaking her head, 'they all work with money.'

Later they go through the apartment, tidying, blowing out candles and gathering glasses. Someone will come at night to clean, Clarissa tells Joanna when she asks about it. In the living room, they help themselves to drinks and sit on one of the couches.

'How did you find out about "O"?' Joanna says to Clarissa, and Clarissa smiles.

'Mr. Stephens. You've met him?' Joanna nods. 'An old boyfriend of mine was a client of his.'

'Client?' Joanna asks, puzzled.

'Yeah. He's a lawyer, you know.' She hadn't known. 'One day I went to see him. I wasn't sure why I was there, but I was just drawn to him. Mesmerized, I guess.' She shakes her head, smiling. 'He did the most amazing things to me. I wanted to stay there forever. Then he took me to meet Pauline.'

Joanna, watching her, is suddenly struck by her beauty, the flaming hair against Clarissa's pale and creamy skin, the sparkling eyes. This woman is happy, she thinks abruptly. This woman is happy with her life.

'You like working for "O",' Joanna says, a statement posed as a question.

'Oh yes,' she laughs. 'I think I was born to work for "O". In two years there has only been one bad experience, otherwise it's all been good. Like today.'

What was the bad experience, Joanna wants to know. She shifts on the couch and faces Clarissa.

'There was this one man,' Clarissa says, shrugging. 'He was getting a little heavy with the whip, using it on my breasts and against my crotch. He was really starting to hurt me.'

'What did you do?' Joanna asks, alarmed.

'I just said "This session is over. I want to go." And he untied me and I left.'

'Just like that?'

'Of course!' Clarissa laughs, then, seriously, she turns to Joanna. 'All of these men are in thrall to Pauline, Joanna. You're very safe. She could destroy them, you know. Anyway, I told her about it and she called him up and told him that if he ever contacted "O" again she would call the press.'

'The press?' Joanna says, and Clarissa grins.

'He was,' she says, sarcastically, 'an elected official.'

'Oh,' Joanna says.

'I kept the money, though.' Clarissa continues. 'I felt I'd earned it, my tits hurt for a week. Actually, Pauline gave me all of the money for that session, her share too. She felt so bad about it. Oh, that reminds me . . .' She reaches into her bag and hands Joanna a white envelope. 'For you,' she says. Joanna takes it.

'Do you still see Mr. Stephens?' Joanna asks her.

'Yes,' Clarissa smiles. 'Quite a lot, actually. He calls me up and orders me to come over to his house. I always go. He's a fascinating man.'

'Does he pay you?' Joanna asks, but Clarissa shakes her head.

'Why should he? He does it for me.' She laughs aloud. 'Maybe I should pay him!' Joanna smiles.

Rising, they gather their things and lock the apartment door. Clarissa says goodbye outside, disappearing into a subway station. Joanna steps to the curb to find a taxi and begin making her way back through the steamy summer afternoon: back through the streets to the station, the train, and the long ride home to her other life in the suburbs.

Chapter Sixteen

Joanna waits beneath a restaurant awning. It is a warm summer day, clear and bright, nearly one o'clock. Dressed as she is in a sober blue dress and low, sensible heels, she looks like several of the serious businesswomen who brush past her into the restaurant, taking no notice. Joanna's black metal bracelet glitters at her wrist, catching the sunlight.

Her hand is warmly taken. 'Joanna,' a voice says, and she turns. The man is broad but thin, dressed conservatively in a dark summer suit. Grey hair bristles over his scalp, cut close. Joanna notices his eyebrows, grey and bushy, nearly meeting in the middle.

'Hello,' she smiles. His name is Mr. Carpenter. At least, that is the name she has been given.

'It's so good to see you,' he says, his voice low and intimate. 'I'm so pleased you could have lunch with me. And don't you look lovely!' He smiles, appraising her. 'Shall we go in?'

He holds the heavy door for her and she steps inside. Joanna feels his warm hand at the small of her back, guiding her forward. Almost immediately the maitre d', a small balding man, looks up and smiles with recognition. Mr. Carpenter greets him by name and the two shake hands. 'You're looking well, Jean Louis,' he says. 'I hope our table is ready.'

'Of course,' the maitre d' nods. 'A booth. As you asked.'

He beckons for them to follow and they walk behind him into the main room of the restaurant. It is crowded with tables of men in business suits, a few women scattered among them. Everyone seems deep in conference, and the room hums with the buzz of money and intrigue. Power lunches, Joanna thinks absently, remembering a phrase she has read somewhere. Several heads nod in greeting to Mr. Carpenter as they pass along a wall lined with booths. Near the middle of the wall, Jean Louis indicates their own table, and Joanna slips behind it onto the plush, slippery bench. Mr. Carpenter settles himself beside her, and they are each handed a menu.

'We have a lovely trout,' he informs them. 'And quail today, grilled with berries.' Turning to Mr. Carpenter, he asks, 'Your usual wine?'

'Please,' says Mr. Carpenter. The small man turns briskly and hurries away. Joanna feels Mr. Carpenter's eyes on her face and she turns, smiling, to him.

'I think you will enjoy your meal,' he says softly, after a moment.

'I'm sure I shall,' Joanna says. 'It's so tedious, always discussing business in an office. Don't you agree?'

He nods, thoughtfully. 'Yes. It would be so much nicer if we could make ourselves more comfortable.'

He pauses, his gaze steady on her face. 'For instance, this is a lovely dress you're wearing. You high-powered women dress so beautifully for the office. But,' he asks, concerned, 'are you quite comforta-ble? Perhaps you'd like to find the ladies' room and freshen up. Your bra must be restrictive. Why don't you remove it?'

'What a wonderful idea,' Joanna says, rising. 'That's very thoughtful of you.' She edges out of the booth and walks back through the restaurant to the lobby, where she finds the bathroom. Inside, a middle-aged woman in a suit applies lipstick in front of the mirror, pursing and blotting her mouth. Joanna goes into one of the stalls and unbuttons her dress, then slips it off her shoulders and takes off her bra, stuffing it into her purse. When she has readjusted her dress, she returns to the table.

'Here,' Joanna says, opening her purse and press-ing the white lace into his hand beneath the table. 'Why don't you keep this for me.'

He thanks her. Clicking open the briefcase beside him in the booth, he puts it inside.

Holding her menu in front of her, Joanna reaches up to unbutton the top button of her dress, pulling the material slightly away from her and angling it so that Mr. Carpenter will be able to just make out the curve of her breast, the shadow of her nipple. She hears his intake of breath, appreciative.

'I suggest the trout,' he tells her when the waiter arrives to take their order. Joanna looks up.

'Trout would be lovely,' she smiles, handing him her menu. Mr. Carpenter asks for his 'usual veal'. The waiter retreats.

'I want you to know,' he says when they are alone, 'that I've been watching you and I'm delighted with the job you're doing. You are a credit to the company, you know.'

'Thank you. I enjoy my work.'

'And you're very good at it.'

'May I say,' she tells him, 'that I respect you very much. You are a model for me, in my career. In fact, you're one of the reasons I chose this kind of work.'

'I'm delighted,' he smiles. Joanna feels a brush of warmth beneath the tablecloth, his hand comfortably resting on her thigh. 'It's nice to know that you career-minded women still look up to hardened businessmen like us.'

'But we have so much to learn from you,' Joanna exclaims. His hand brushes softly over her lap.

'And we from you,' he says.

Joanna folds her hands in front of her on the table-top. She shifts slightly on the bench, turning her knees towards him, making herself more accessible. Immediately, she feels his hand coast down her lap to her knees, touching the bare skin, gently easing them apart. Above the table, his other hand casually fingers his wineglass.

'What do you think the market's doing?' Mr. Carpenter asks. Joanna takes a sip of her wine.

'Soft,' she says carefully, her lips wet with wine. 'At least, it's been soft for a time. But now,' Joanna smiles, 'I think it will get hard.' She leans slightly forward. 'Very hard,' she confides, whispering.

'You may be right,' he tells her. The hand dips beneath her dress, sliding easily between her thighs. Joanna separates them slightly. She resists the urge to pull up her dress. 'Why don't you tell me,' Mr. Carpenter smiles, 'a little bit about yourself.'

Joanna smiles. 'Would you like to know what I love most about our business?' she asks. 'The issues of control. You see,' she reclines lightly against the back of the booth as his fingers brush the silk of her underpants, 'we work so hard. We strain for something, some specific goal. Yes? But all the time there are these other pressures, other elements, making us behave in other ways. Making us do things we would never do of our own volition. So even as we're straining for something, yearning for it, these other pressures are manipulating us, taking control of us. That's what I love,' Joanna sighs. His hand is damp between her thighs. 'I love the being out of control.'

'I quite agree,' Mr. Carpenter says, nodding.

The waiter brings their lunch, settling two

steaming plates before them. Mr. Carpenter's hand returns to the tabletop and lifts his wineglass. 'To this meeting,' he smiles at Joanna. They clink.

'Perhaps,' he says, 'before we begin our lunch, you'd like to visit the ladies' room again. I'm very worried about your comfort,' he frowns. 'I wouldn't want anything to stand in its way.'

'How kind,' Joanna says. Smoothing down her dress, she climbs out of the booth and walks through the restaurant again, feeling Mr. Carpenter's gaze at her back. In the bathroom, she removes her underpants.

'For you,' she says, returning. 'A small gift, to show my appreciation. I want to thank you for everything you're doing on my behalf.'

'Not at all,' he tells her, accepting the damp silk under the tablecloth. He slips it into his briefcase. 'It's a pleasure.'

Joanna takes a bite of her trout, which is flaky and light. 'How fresh!' she says brightly. Mr. Carpenter's hand has returned to her thighs, easing up her dress. 'One can almost imagine it swimming, undulating through the currents of a river, slippery and wriggling.'

'Do you enjoy imagining that?' He asks. His fingers part her thighs and run lightly over the crack of her cunt, making her catch her breath.

'Oh yes,' she sighs. 'Sometimes I feel just like a fish myself, very wet and very slippery. Sometimes I feel like my whole body is swimming, even though I'm doing something else entirely. Working, for example. Or even having lunch in a beautiful restaurant like this.'

'How curious,' he comments, intrigued.

'I love to swim,' Joanna continues, matter of factly. His fingers pull gently at her moist pubic hairs. 'I love the feeling of being lost in waves, and the water sliding all around me.' She takes another bite of her fish. Mr. Carpenter eats deftly with one hand, cutting the tender veal with the side of his fork. 'Do you like to swim?' She asks.

'Not much,' he says. 'But I enjoy diving.'

Joanna moans, barely audibly, as his fingers slips into her cunt, massaging her inside with small strokes.

ELIZABETH BENNETT

'I know what you mean,' she says, regaining control of her face. 'There's a beautiful moment when you pierce the surface of the water and glide down into it, deep into it, submerging yourself.'

'Are you a strong swimmer?' Mr. Carpenter asks. The heel of his hand finds the top of Joanna's cunt, lightly pressing it as his finger moves inside her. 'What sort of stroke do you prefer? A slow crawl, perhaps?'

'Mmm,' she says, eyes closed, as if she is trying to remember. 'I like the breast stroke very much, especially when the current is slow and the water is warm. It feels good to be on top of the water, carried by it, lifted up.' Joanna shifts slightly, letting him sink further inside. She feels his finger quicken, the heel of his hand slick and hard against her, and knows she is about to come. 'But when the waves get faster and stronger, I like the rhythm of the crawl, the way my thighs move in the currents, faster and faster, and I wish I could keep it going forever.'

'So do I,' Mr. Carpenter whispers. 'You make it sound very beautiful.'

'Yes . . . beautiful,' Joanna gasps, wincing briefly as she comes, streaming over his hand. She reaches for her napkin and covers her face, holding it against her nose.

The hand between her thighs is still. Then, slowly, it glides out of her and down her legs, leaving a wet and sticky trail.

'God bless,' says Mr. Carpenter, his face sympathetic.

'Such a nasty cold,' says Joanna. 'But thank you.'

The waiter takes their plates. 'Would you like dessert?' asks Mr. Carpenter. 'They have some fine things here.'

She turns to smile at him. 'Something sweet?' Joanna considers. 'I don't think so. Perhaps I've had enough already. But what about you?' Silently, her own hand slips beneath the table and into his lap, gently squeezing him. He is, to Joanna's surprise, only moderately hard, and it crosses her mind that he has already come.

'No,' say Mr. Carpenter. 'I'm grateful for the suggestion, but really I must be getting back to the office. These business lunches are lovely, but one mustn't forget where one's real work lies.'

'Of course one mustn't,' Joanna agrees, nodding solemnly.

Outside, in front of the restaurant, he touches her face and kisses her tenderly on both cheeks, two business associates saying goodbye, their minds already elsewhere. She catches her own scent on his fingers. When he leaves, Joanna turns in the opposite direction and walks to a nearby department store where Curtis has given her an account. Her closets at home in the suburbs are full of beautiful clothes, but she has recently found herself in desperate need of more underwear.

Chapter Seventeen

Dr. Simon's office is off the marbled lobby of an apartment building on the east side of the park, not far from the restaurant where Joanna first observed then later met with Pauline. It is mid-afternoon, an overcast Wednesday. Joanna's heels click sharply over the marble as she crosses it to the heavy marble door marked with a plaque: OB-GYN. She rings the bell and waits, automatically reaching up to check the knotted hair at her nape.

He comes to let her in, a short, thickset man with thin ash-colored hair, in his fifties, Joanna guesses. He wears a white medical jacket over his trousers and shirt, a stethoscope protruding from the breast pocket, all very official. 'Please come in,' he says, his voice careful with the smooth intonation of doctors. Joanna steps inside. The reception area and waiting room are dark. 'This way,' Dr. Simon beckons, stepping in front of her. She follows him to the end of the hall into an office, where they take seats on the opposite sides of a heavy desk.

'I'm so grateful you could see me, Doctor,' Joanna says, clutching her purse on her lap.

'Not at all,' he nods, his face grim. 'That's what I'm here for.' Behind him, a door opens and a younger man in a white coat enters. He leans awkwardly against the wall, next to Dr. Simon's chair, and crosses his arms.

'This is Dr. Stein,' Dr. Simon is saying. 'He is a medical student. I've asked him to observe our consultation, and later, the examination. You have no objection?'

'Oh, of course not,' Joanna exclaims.

The two men watch her silently for a moment. Joanna glances around the room, shelves of books, framed prints on the walls. Several silver picture frames on the desk have, she notices, been turned face down. She suppresses a smile.

'Let's begin with some general questions,' Dr. Simon says, interrupting her thoughts. His hands are folded on the desk in front of him, an expression of slight concern on his face. 'Your age?'

'Twenty-eight,' Joanna says.

'And how long have you been sexually active?'

Sexually active? Joanna thinks. 'Oh,' she blushes, 'not very long. I've had a boyfriend for about a year now.'

'And how often do you have sex,' he asks.

She looks up, considering. 'All the time,' Joanna sighs. 'At least once every month.'

He nods, serious. 'Please describe it for me. The basic pattern of it.' He pauses, taking in Joanna's confused expression. 'I'll need to know this, in order to help you,' he says kindly.

'Well,' she says carefully. 'First he takes me to

dinner, then usually to a movie. Then we go back to his apartment. He sits on the couch and I stand in front of him and he watches me take off my clothes.'

'All of your clothes?'

'Yes,' Joanna nods, blushing. 'Then I turn around so that I'm facing away from him, and get down on my hands and knees. I can hear him behind me, unzipping his pants and taking out his . . . you know.'

'Cock,' Dr. Simon says shortly. He shifts uncomfortably on his leather chair.

'Yes, that. Then he gets behind me and, you know, puts it in and sort of pushes it in and out. And then a minute later he sort of hisses, like somebody punched him or something. Then that's it.'

The medical student unfolds his arms and puts his hands in his pockets. 'Excuse me for interrupting,' he says, glancing at Dr. Simon, 'but does your boyfriend touch your breasts?'

'No,' Joanna shakes her head, looking confused. 'Is he supposed to?'

'Not necessarily,' Dr. Simon says authoritatively. 'But some women find it pleasurable.'

'Really?' Joanna frowns.

'Yes,' he says dismissively. 'But tell me, exactly what is the nature of your problem?'

Joanna blushes. 'It's so embarrassing.'

'That's all right,' says Dr. Simon. 'We're both doctors. We're here to help you.'

'Oh I know!' Joanna cries. 'I'm so grateful. It's just . . . it's just so hard to talk about.'

'Take your time,' says Dr. Stein, the medical student.

'Well,' she begins, her head down. 'I was wondering, you know, if there might be something wrong with me. Some medical reason why . . . why I can't, you know . . .'

'Come,' says Dr. Simon. 'You would like me to examine you, in order to see if there is a physiological obstacle.'

'Yes,' Joanna nods enthusiastically. 'Oh would you? Please examine me thoroughly. My boyfriend is so upset about this, and of course, so am I.'

'You would like to come, in other words.'

'Oh yes, yes, I would,' Joanna says. 'But there must be something wrong. I mean, he's doing everything right, isn't he?'

The two doctors exchange glances. 'We'll have a look,' Dr. Simon says, rising. 'We'll see what we can find.'

He leads Joanna into an adjoining examining room and points to a screen. 'Please take off all of your clothes,' he says.

'You mean my bra too?' She asks. 'And my panties?'

'Yes,' he nods, impassive. 'I'm afraid so. There is a gown over the chair. Please put it on so that it ties in front. I will be back in a minute and we will begin the examination.'

He turns, shutting the door behind him. Through it she hears muffled voices, a laugh. Joanna wonders briefly if either of them is really a doctor. Not that it matters, she smiles to herself.

She goes behind the screen and removes her clothes, unhooking her bra and peeling off her underpants. Then she slips on the gown, made of some kind of soft paper, white. It crinkles as she fumbles with the ties down her front. She goes to the leather examining table and sits sideways on it, waiting. Before her, a steel table is covered with examining tools, white cotton swabs, syringes, lubricant and rubber surgical tubing. The door opens.

'All set?' Dr. Simon asks brightly. 'Please lie back on the table. Just relax.'

Joanna lies back, her legs together, her hands demurely crossed over her stomach. On her forearm, the black metal bracelet glitters dark against the pale of her skin. Dr. Simon goes to the foot of the table. The medical student stands at Joanna's head, watching.

'Just scoot down a bit, that's right,' Dr. Simon croons as Joanna moves down the table towards him. Her ass rests at its edge. He gently lifts her legs and moves them apart, settling her heels in the cold steel stirrups. Then, to her surprise, she feels something move across her ankles and tighten, locking her in place. 'This is for your own protection,' he tells her. 'It's important that you do not move. Please try to relax. I know this is difficult for you.'

'Oh, it is,' Joanna says fearfully. 'Will it hurt?'

'I hope not,' Dr. Simon says, sympathetically. 'I'll try to make you as comfortable as possible. Dr. Stein? Will you help me with the screen please?'

Together they take a long piece of green surgical draping and place it across Joanna's stomach, then, lifting two of its corners, they hook it overhead to tall steel poles. When they are finished, there is a wall of green between Joanna's upper and lower half. Her spread legs, her heels cold in the stirrups, her rapidly dampening cunt are all out of sight behind it. She sighs, closing her eyes. Joanna's wrists are lifted and stretched above her head. She feels the supple rubber of surgical tubing being wrapped around her wrists, not too tight. Then they are fastened to something unseen at the end of the examining table. The two men stand over her for a moment, their eyes on Joanna's face and the soft bulges of her breasts beneath the white paper.

'Let's begin,' says Dr. Simon.

Slowly, he begins to unfasten the paper gown, untying each knot then moving to the next, his fingers lightly tracing the visible inch of skin down her body. When the last tie is undone, he carefully spreads the gown apart, bunching it against her sides, then stands solemnly, examining her breasts. 'Please watch carefully, Dr. Stein,' he says. He leans over her slightly. Joanna, looking at the ceiling, feels his palm softly press the underside of one of her breasts, gently pushing it up. With his other hand he lightly brushes the upper part of the breast, softly, with his fingertips, avoiding the nipple. Over and over in slightly decreasing arcs, bringing his fingers closer to the hard and throbbing point. Joanna, forgetting herself, moans quietly. 'Try to relax,' he mutters.

Finally, the fingers reach her nipple and glide over it, teasing it, then pressing it. He rolls it firmly but clinically between two fingers, his face only inches away from it now. Then, straightening up, he asks for something from the steel table across the room. Joanna hears the squelch of a tube, then something cool at the edge of her breast. 'This shouldn't hurt,' he tells her calmly, beginning to rub lubrication over her skin, everywhere but against the nipple. Warm palms massage her breast, smooth and firm, unhurried. Then the flesh is squeezed between them, pushing it straight up. Joanna, glancing down, can see the dark tip rising above his fingers. Dr. Simon bends down and tentatively begins to lick it. Joanna groans loudly, loving the rasp of his tongue, the warm and sticky palms holding her steady beneath his mouth. At her head, the medical student places a comforting hand on her shoulder. 'Just relax,' he tells her, trying to sound professional. Joanna, nonetheless, hears a wisp of urgency in his voice. She moans again, aware of intense heat between her legs.

Dr. Simon sucks her nipple, rhythmically, his tongue gliding over it inside his mouth. She hears his sounds and she gasps, her eyes shut, rolling her head back and forth. The medical student's hand is cold on her shoulder. She wants to cry out. The mouth sucks and sucks. She feels the blunt edge of teeth lightly bite down and groans, almost in pain. He straightens up.

'Dr Stein,' he says calmly, 'would you like to examine the other breast?'

The cold hand leaves her shoulder and moves down, fumbling through the same process on Joanna's other side. The breast is touched and felt, lubricant is massaged over it, then her nipple is firmly sucked and licked and nearly bitten. When he has finished, he looks up expectantly at the older man, who briefly nods, then turns to Joanna. He looks carefully at her, taking in the flushed cheeks and quickened breath, but says nothing. Then, finally, he tells her that she will now be examined internally, that they will try not to hurt her, that, again she should relax, try to relax and remember: they are doctors.

'Yes,' Joanna says. 'Oh yes, I will.'

They move down the table and disappear behind the green curtain. She hears the roll of steel balls, a chair being wheeled between her spread legs. Then breath, warm and quick over her crotch as a body settles itself on the chair. Professional fingers spread her, and she can almost feel the eyes, looking and looking. She imagines hands, folding back the outer lips, a head between them, drawing close, almost touching. Joanna holds her breath.

Then, a warm mouth swallows her, lightly pushing the ridges aside and back again. The sound of suction. The mouth makes small movements to left and right. Joanna presses against it, spreading her legs even farther, as far as she can. 'Oh please,' she whispers. A damp hand pats her inner thighs, comforting. The mouth continues to suck. Joanna thinks of whirling, falling. Slowly she climbs to the edge of coming but holds herself back.

Abruptly, a shift of weight. The mouth recedes and, a minute later, she is penetrated by something thick and pulsing. Hips push between her legs, pull back, then push again. A hand tangles in her pubic hair, massaging the flesh beneath it. He fucks her quickly, then, thrusting hard. She wonders which one it is, then hears a moan, and knows. He comes a few seconds later, crying out 'Yes . . . Yes . . .' and slowly pulls away. Immediately, another body takes his place and Joanna feels the dull slide of a longer cock, smoothly entering her, beginning to pound.

Dr. Simon steps from behind the curtain and comes to the head of the table, touching her forehead, taking in the rapt contortion of her face. Leaning down, he kisses her deeply, offering her his tongue to suck and Joanna sucks it, frantically, tasting herself. She feels his hand drift to her breast, twisting the nipple, then the other breast, back and forth between them. Between her legs, the urgency of heat and rhythm, a high-pitched wail growing louder. She arches into the hands at her breasts, tries to thrust with her hips letting it enter her deeply. When his climax begins she lets her own devour her, shooting down to the steel-encased heels and up again, flooding her cunt. Her scream rushes over the tongue in her mouth, down his throat. Dimly, a soothing hand pats her breast. The unseen cock pulls slowly out.

Dr. Simon releases her mouth and straightens up, his hand still cool on her forehead. 'There, there,' he croons. 'It wasn't too painful, my dear, and now it's over. I think,' he says, 'we may have found your problem.'

Joanna gushes with gratitude until she is drenched.

Chapter Eighteen

Joanna is dressing for a party, this time in one of her own conservative silk dresses. It falls smoothly over her breasts, baring only the upper part of her chest, and gathers at her waist in dark green folds before falling to well below her knees. She clasps pearls, a gift from Curtis, behind her neck, just below the knotted coil of her hair.

Passing her open door, he leans in and watches approvingly. 'You look lovely,' Curtis says. 'Just beautiful. I won't be a minute.' She hears him pad down the hall to his own room and begin to change out of his business suit into something more appropriate.

Joanna dislikes these evenings. The civilized chatter of Curtis's friends, the pretentious splendor of the large suburban houses where they gather to drink and eat. The women are groomed and preserved, their hair tastefully dyed to minimize the grey without denying its existence. They wear good jewelry, family things with small but impressive stones. Always, they condescend to Joanna, calling her 'such a sweet girl', and 'Curtis's young wife.' It is not, she knows, that she is being singled out for special attention. Curtis is only one of several among his friends who have married young, sometimes extremely young girls, and it is this very phenomenon, this trend, which so irritates and threatens the hostesses.

Tonight's party promises to be especially odious, Martha and Trevor are celebrating an anniversary, their thirty-fifth, and will be expecting both approbation and envy from their guests. Trevor, Joanna knows, has something to do with Curtis's bank, and 'goes way back' with her husband, to college, to prep school, perhaps even farther. Martha is a maddeningly tireless raiser of funds for various tasteful causes, a joiner, a member, a sitter on boards. More than once, she has pointedly asked Joanna if she might spare some free time for this or that. Joanna has always said she would try, then never returned Martha's calls. Martha, Joanna suspects, has little regard for women of leisure.

In the car, Curtis fiddles with the radio, looking for classical. The ride is brief, along the coast and then up into the hills on the far edge of their suburb. Joanna sits with her hands calmly folded in her lap. 'Thoughtful,' she hears him say.

'What?'

'You're thoughtful tonight,' he says, his voice kind.

'Oh, not really,' she smiles, touching his knee. 'It's just that I was thinking about Martha, and all that work she does. Maybe I should volunteer for something.'

'If you like,' he comments. 'Only if you feel the need for it. Don't do it on my account.' She turns to look at his face, a dark silhouette. 'I love the idea of you at home, really,' he muses. 'Reading, sitting out on the porch. Waiting for me. Just being beautiful. But,' he goes on, 'I wouldn't stand in your way, of course, if you did want to do some volunteer work.'

'Of course,' Joanna says. 'I know. Well, I'll think about it.'

They pass through the tall stone gate and head up the driveway. Martha and Trevor live in what they themselves refer to as 'a pile', old and huge and somber. A mansion, Joanna thinks, pulling up in front of it. A valet unlocks her door and she climbs out.

Inside, she hands the maid their anniversary gift, a crystal vase clearly marked with the name of the store so that Martha can easily return it, as Joanna knows she will. Trevor is visible in the crowded living room off the entryway, booming with laughter, holding a bottle of champagne. Curtis's arm creeps around Joanna's shoulders. Somewhere a band plays swing tunes.

'There you are,' a voice cries. Martha descends the stairs, her expression a flawless approximation of pleasure. She wears black silk and major jewelry, Joanna thinks. Diamonds at her throat, sapphires in her ears, more diamonds at her wrists.

'You look sensational,' Curtis is saying. He cups her chin familiarly in his hand and turns to Joanna. 'Is this the face of a woman who's been married for thirty-five years?' he asks, grinning.

'This is the face,' Joanna says carefully, smiling, 'of a woman who's been *happily* married for thirty-five years.'

Curtis smiles approvingly. Martha leans forward. 'Joanna,' she says, kissing her cheek, 'how sweet of you to come. That green is very becoming on you.'

'Thank you,' Joanna says. 'And many congratulations on your anniversary.' She coils her arm through Curtis's.

'Oh go on in,' Martha cries as the front door rings behind them. 'Have some champagne. Trevor is in there somewhere, at least, I assume he is. Go and find him for me and tell him to make sure everyone has a drink. Darling!' she shouts, turning to the new arrival. Joanna and Curtis, dismissed, enter the living room.

Everyone's here, Joanna thinks, glumly surveying the crowd. The cared-for grey heads of the women, the shining bald heads of the men. Every now and then the abrupt interruption of a young woman: brunette or blonde or redhead, on someone's arm. Curtis takes two glasses from a waiter and hands one to Joanna. He lifts his own in a whispered toast. 'To the face of a woman who's been happily married for two years,' he says, clinking. Joanna smiles and sips.

Almost immediately, the wave of acquaintances begins, coming in twos and threes to greet them. Colleagues from the bank, friends like Trevor, from 'way back', people whose faces are familiar from other parties in other homes. Joanna smiles and nods until her face feels stiff, frozen with the effort of looking interested. She kisses Trevor on his flushed and fleshy cheeks, congratulates him, permits his own exuberant and lengthy hug, his large hands at her lower back.

Martha, hushing the swing band, announces dinner and slowly the wave of guests begins to move towards the door, onto a patio strung with lanterns. Curtis finds their table almost immediately, not far from the door, and holds Joanna's chair for her. She sits, examining the beauty of the setting: flowers and silver and china. The table is set for six.

Behind her, Curtis's voice rises in pleasure, greeting a friend. 'You're sitting here?' He says. 'Good, you're finally going to meet my wife. Joanna,' Curtis says, 'here's someone I'd like you to meet.'

Sighing, Joanna rises and turns, then feels herself go white. 'Barton,' Curtis is saying, 'my wife Joanna. Joanna this is Barton Stephens, my old friend, and, incidentally, my lawyer.'

'Oh,' Joanna whispers, staring. He leans slightly foward.

'Joanna,' Mr. Stephens says quietly, pressing her hand. 'I can't tell you what a delight it is to meet you at last. Now, Curtis has always told me how lovely you were, but I never imagined.'

'Thank you,' says Joanna, trembling. She can't tear her eyes from his. Curtis pulls back her chair again.

'Sweetheart?' he says. Joanna lowers herself, steadying herself against the table.

The others take their seats, Curtis beside Joanna, Mr. Stephens on his far side. Joanna is grateful for that, at least. The two men begin to discuss Trevor and Martha, then quickly move on to politics, commerce, real estate. The woman on Joanna's other side is young and vibrant, an advertising executive responsible, she tells Joanna, for a major series of well-known television commercials. 'What do you do?' She asks politely.

'Nothing much,' Joanna says. 'I don't really have a career.'

'Oh,' the woman says uncomfortably, changing the subject.

When the main course has been finished and their plates cleared away, there are a series of toasts

168

extolling the virtues of marriage, longevity, security. Joanna automatically raises her glass and drinks, each time, numbly feeling the cool champagne slide down her throat. The band begins to play.

'Well, Curtis,' a familiar voice says, 'I would like permission to dance with your wife.'

'Fine with me,' Curtis says, raising his hands.

Mr. Stephens gets to his feet and looks down at her expectantly. 'I'd be honored,' he says simply.

'Watch him,' she hears her husband laugh. 'He's a devil!'

Joanna gets up and lets him lead her to the dance floor. He is a good dancer, his hand firm around her waist. Joanna is awkward in his arms, shaking and stumbling.

'Well, well,' he says, his voice intimate at her ear.

'Please don't tell him,' Joanna cries, gripping his shoulder with her hand. 'Please, please don't tell him.'

'My dear,' he laughs, 'I have no intention of telling him. You have a secret. I like secrets, secrets are powerful. I enjoy power.'

'I know,' she moans. 'I know.'

He is silent for a moment, bending her to the music. Briefly, she feels his cheek press her own. 'I've known Curtis for a long time, you know,' Mr. Stephens says. 'He has secrets of his own.'

Joanna pushes herself back and looks at him carefully. 'I don't give a damn about his secrets.' Her voice is fierce. 'Just don't tell him mine. Promise me.'

'I give you my word,' he smiles. The song ends and there is polite clapping. Joanna looks around for Curtis. 'Another?' Mr. Stephens asks politely as the music starts again. Sighing, Joanna takes his hand and they begin to move. 'And you, dear Joanna,' he whispers. 'How are you getting on?'

'I'm fine,' she hisses. Then, a little cruelly, 'I met your friend Clarissa.'

'Ah,' he smiles down at her, 'such a sweet girl. I find her very stimulating.'

'I'm sure you do,' Joanna says, letting him pull her close. A hand lands on her shoulder.

'Enough already,' Curtis laughs. 'How long can a man be expected to calmly sit by and watch somebody else dance with his wife?'

'Of course,' says Mr. Stephens, bowing gallantly. 'Joanna, it's been a pleasure. I certainly hope we'll meet again.'

'Yes, I hope so,' Joanna says, trying to smile. Curtis takes her hand and she leans against him, moving to the music.

'This is so nice,' he is saying, his voice soft at her ear. 'Would you like to have a party for our next anniversary?'

'That would be lovely,' Joanna sighs, hating the very notion. 'But three years hardly carries the weight of thirty-five, you know.'

'It does with me,' he smiles, patting her back.

When the song ends she turns to him and asks, hesitantly, if they can go. 'I don't actually feel very well,' Joanna says. 'I think, that venison for dinner . . . Would you mind?'

'Of course,' he says. 'Of course, my dear. I'll go and say goodbye then, shall I?'

'Yes,' Joanna says, grateful. She returns to the table for her bag. Mr. Stephens isn't there, she is relieved to see. She moves quickly, hoping to escape without seeing him again, but as she is leaving the patio, her arm folded into her husband's, he catches her eye from the edge of the crowd and holds it, intent, his mouth folded in an expression of pleasure and control – an expression, as it happens, that Joanna remembers very well.

Chapter Nineteen

She wears black high heeled shoes, black stockings hooked to a garter belt, a glittering black bracelet at her wrist, no bra, no underpants. She wears a summer dress, demure and oddly pale against the black of her stockings and shoes. She rings the doorbell. It is two o'clock exactly, a summer afternoon in the city.

The door is answered by a servant, a beautiful young woman, Asian. She beckons, silent, and Joanna follows her through a sitting room and down a hall where she gestures at a closed door, then turns away. Joanna enters.

The bull-necked man from the party is sitting in a plush armchair, wrapped in a heavy silk robe. His hands fondle the long black whip across his lap. He does not look up when she enters. 'Come in,' he says, his voice low. 'Stand in front of me. Face me.'

Joanna does, her feet together, her eyes on the floor. At the edge of her vision, she is aware of his hand, lovingly caressing the whip. For a long moment, he is silent.

'I asked to see you,' he says finally, 'because of your behavior when we last met. I did not have an opportunity to discipline you then, but I have been asked to discipline you now, and I shall. Do you have anything to say for yourself?'

'Please don't hurt me,' Joanna whimpers. 'I'm sorry I misbehaved.'

'That may be,' the bull-necked man says. 'But you're not sorry enough. When I'm finished with you, you'll be sorry enough.'

Joanna says nothing. 'Take off your dress,' she hears him growl.

Meekly, her eyes on the floor, Joanna unzips her dress. It falls to the floor and she steps away from it and stands, her legs slightly apart. She feels his gaze at her breasts and crotch, then hears the crinkle of silk, his knees parting beneath the robe. 'Get on your hands and knees and come here,' he says.

Slowly, Joanna kneels and crawls, the carpet rough against her legs and palms. As she approaches him, the man leans back into the deep chair, parts his knees and raises them until his feet rest on the cushion, spreading himself for her. His cock and scrotum are limp against his thigh. A hand reaches into her hair and pulls, burying her face between his legs. 'Lick me,' he says calmly. 'You little cunt.'

Joanna begins to lick his balls, tenderly, but he pulls harder, smearing her face with them. She tries to breath. With his other hand, he lightly taps her buttock with the long whip, just to let her know it's there. 'Lower,' the voice says. 'Lick my ass.'

She does, tentatively at first, then, convinced he is at least scrupulously clean, with her whole tongue. His breath rasps. The whip drums softly on her skin. His cock stiffens with the rush of blood, pulsing slightly. Suddenly he pulls her head back sharply, the hand rough in her hair, and takes hold of himself. 'Open your mouth,' he says. Joanna parts her lips and lets her jaw relax.

He is massaging himself, inches from her face, sliding his hand tightly from root to tip, his eyes on her, watching. He reaches his climax quickly. Joanna thinks he will pull her mouth down over the cock, smack her, turn over and penetrate her, something, but the man calmly shoots into her mouth, not even touching it but taking his pleasure from her own alarm. 'Swallow,' he hisses when he is done. Joanna gulps and swallows, choking.

For a minute, he says nothing. Then he is on his feet, his hand twisting her hair and yanking her up, turning her, pushing her across the room. The whip trails behind him in his other hand. 'Move, bitch,' he shouts. 'Now get on your knees.' Joanna kneels. She is between two posts of dark wood about five feet apart, thick and strong, with chains attached to them and dangling down. Metal clicks over her wrists, fastening her hands apart and slightly raised. Then, to her surprise, a thick rope is coiled around her right leg and attached to something a foot or two behind her, then the other leg, and she is suddenly spread apart and forced to lean slightly forward, like a four-legged animal in the act of rearing up. He steps away from her. Behind her, a door opens, the sound of a light tread.

Into the field of her vision, the Asian woman walks softly, dressed now as Joanna is dressed in garter and stockings and heels, but there is something new, something Joanna had not noticed before: a black metal bracelet at her wrist. Her face is calm. Her small breasts swing slightly as she walks in front of Joanna and kneels, facing her, a few feet away.

Behind her, the bull-necked man has watched without comment, but now Joanna hears the whistle of his whip, testing the air, and braces herself. Instead, she feels a soft hand at the back of her neck, smoothing her hair forward, baring her shoulders, then gliding down, a finger along her spine.

She shivers. The finger slips between her buttocks and stops at the anus, which tightens involuntarily. He pushes slightly, causing pressure. 'Please,' Joanna says.

Immediately, he whips her, the leather cracking against her skin. She yelps with pain but it only excites him. The whip falls through the air, over and over, blanketing her buttocks, then her thighs, with heat. She wants to cry. 'You're hurting me,' she howls, forgetting that this is exactly what he wants, forgetting that this will only make him want to hurt her more. He steps behind her and continues, the strokes now up and angled, whipping her inner thighs, almost to the crotch. Joanna sags forward, whimpering, moaning at each blow, her head down. When he pauses, she breathes deeply, feeling the sting of her new welts. Through the pain, she feels his hands, moist now with lubricant, coating her ass and thighs, firmly rubbing the ring of muscle around her anus.

He thrusts something into her face and she squints, focusing. Long and slender, a phallus made of plastic, she thinks, or hard rubber. 'Lick this,' the man says, almost kindly. Joanna licks it briefly, then stops, hearing his laugh. 'You'd better get it wetter than that,' he sneers. 'It's going straight up your ass.'

Involuntarily, she gasps, meeting the eyes of the Asian woman, which give back nothing. 'No,' Joanna says. A fierce hand seizes her cunt, squeezing it cruelly.

'Lick it,' says the bull-necked man. Joanna closes her eyes and licks, drenching it.

Long fingers spread her buttocks. The phallus is rubbed hard against her anus, then pressed. Joanna feels the shock of its penetration and glide. She groans, fighting it, but it only hurts more. Her hands are tight in the manacles, the rope rubs her legs, holding them apart. The phallus continues its climb into her bowels, twisting slightly. When it stops, the hand massages her skin around its protruding stump, feeling its hardness through the tissue. She is numbly aware of a finger in her cunt, testing the pressure, the size, the available room. To her surprise, Joanna senses her own wetness.

A hand snaps, the sound echoing loudly through the room. Instantly, the Asian woman leans forward and begins to kiss Joanna, deeply, her tongue gentle. Joanna, shocked at first, tries to pull back from the open mouth but a hand at the back of her own head holds her steady and, to drive the point home, the whip lands sharply on her thighs. She lets her eyes close and tries to drift. The tongue feeding in her mouth is feathery and soft. She feels the bull-necked man step around to her side.

Abruptly, he pulls them apart, his hands grasping their hair, and steps close so that his stiffening cock is pushed between their mouths. 'Get me hard,' he says simply, and together the two women begin to lick, Joanna at the swinging pouch of his scrotum, the Asian woman running her tongue along the length of it. Slowly the cock begins to harden and jerk.

Breathing hard, he pushes the Asian woman away from him and down, until her face is level with Joanna's breasts where she begins to lick again, solemnly, without sound. Joanna moans, open-mouthed, and the hard cock is promptly inserted between her lips. He holds her head tightly, the movement of his hips slow but deep. Joanna feels on the edge of choking. The Asian woman switches her attention to the other breast, reaching up to finger the first, pressing the nipple softly.

Just before Joanna feels the bull-necked man is about to come, he pulls back from her and steps away. For a moment he merely watches the Asian woman lap at Joanna's breasts, then, quietly, he tells her to lie down, on her back. The woman turns and lies back, her head between Joanna's spread knees. The man stands thoughtfully for a moment, then walks quickly to the other side of the room, returning with objects. He reaches between Joanna's bent legs to lift the head of the other woman, sliding a small, firm cushion beneath it, bringing her mouth only inches below Joanna's open cunt. Joanna gasps at what she knows will happen, and is promptly punished by a cruel hand, twisting her nipple. Between her legs, she feels the tip of a tongue make contact.

The man kneels beside the supine body of the Asian woman, thoughtfully touching the flat breasts and nearly hairless crotch. Then he bends over her and parts her legs to reach between them and rub. His hand comes away wet. Joanna hears a low moan, vibrating into her own cunt. He bends over the woman again, this time with something large in his hand. Joanna's eyes widen at the size of it, the impossibility of it, but the phallus slips almost easily between the parted thighs, disappearing up into her, pushed steadily in. Almost imperceptibly, the woman's hips begin to move, to rock against it. The man gently lifts one of the Asian woman's hands and moves it to her crotch and leaves it there. Immediately, she begins to touch herself, thrusting against the phallus inside her. Another moan emanates into Joanna's crotch.

He moves behind Joanna and kneels, testing her again with his finger then slowly entering her, burying himself, reaching around her front to almost tenderly stroke her breasts. With his hips, he nudges her forward and down until she presses against the mouth of the woman beneath her. The mouth is steady and warm and moving. Joanna has never felt so stretched and so full. At first the pain is intense, but the man is curiously gentle with her, responsive to her sounds, slowing when she groans, continuing when she is silent. Before her, Joanna watches the Asian woman masturbate, arching against her own fingers, thrusting the phallus more deeply inside herself with her other hand, enraptured. Then Joanna becomes aware of her own thrustings, a rhythmic press against the generous, attentive mouth, the gentle probing of the man in her cunt, even the warm sensation of fullness in her rectum. Her breasts quiver and ache. The sound of moaning, her own, she thinks, but isn't sure, then the growl at her ear saying yes, you bitch, now come in her face, and Joanna obeys, feeling his deep spasm inside her, her body erupting in sweetness against the mouth that opens to take it in.

Chapter Twenty

A Monday afternoon, ripe with city heat. Joanna stands on the pavement in front of an elegant downtown hotel, self-consciously fingering the black bracelet at her wrist. Around her, the city swirls with rushing figures and choked, aggravated traffic. The revolving door behind her, the entrance to the hotel, makes a swishing sound as it swallows and disgorges bodies: tourists, visiting businessmen – perhaps, Joanna thinks, smiling, other employees of 'O'. She wears a short black skirt and a white shirt with buttons in front, tucked in. She has been waiting for nearly ten minutes.

A black limousine glides to the curb in front of her and stops. Joanna, who has been told to expect a large limousine, is nonetheless astonished by its size. It is one of those breathtaking automobiles one some- times notices, cruising the wealthier districts near the park or carrying film stars to parties or premiers. One of those automobiles that virtually assures a famous passenger within. The long windows shine black at her, revealing not even a shape or a presence, but the door opens and a young man gets out, stands and turns to look at her, his gaze lingering at her bracelet. He smiles politely. 'Please get in,' he says. Joanna walks to the car and climbs inside.

The interior is huge. Two long benches of leather face each other, five feet apart. A man sits on each one, but Joanna is immediately drawn to the one on her right. He is young, in his thirties perhaps, with black hair hanging thickly to his shoulders. Dressed beautifully in an Italian suit and shirt, he exudes a regal air, an air of privilege and effortless superiority. He smiles at Joanna, gesturing for her to sit across from him, next to the other man. Behind her, the man who held the door for Joanna climbs in after her and sits on her other side.

Briefly, the regal man opposite flicks a switch and speaks to his chauffeur. The car begins to move forward, smooth as velvet. The switch is flicked again and they are silent. Despite the pedestrians wildly peering at the car, trying to see inside, despite the chauffeur who is barely visible through a clouded glass partition, Joanna feels as alone with these three men as if they were all in a locked room.

'I am Rene,' the man across from her says quietly, smiling. 'And you are Joanna.'

'Yes,' Joanna says.

'These men are my bodyguards,' he says, gesturing at them. 'Though for the purposes of this meeting, they have been permitted to show considerably more interest in your body than in mine.' Joanna nods. 'They are very good men,' Rene continues. 'Very gentle, very attentive. I'm sure you will not mind what they will do to you.'

'Of course,' Joanna says.

He pauses, his eyes intent on her face. 'And you,' Rene says, 'are a very beautiful woman.'

Joanna thanks him.

'Many men do not know how to please a beautiful woman,' he continues thoughtfully, 'but you will find that I do.'

'Yes,' Joanna says. 'I think I will.'

He smiles crisply, acknowledging her willingness, her confidence in him, then turns to his men and gives a quick nod.

Gently, Joanna feels their hands on her back and shoulders, easing her down onto the plush leather bench. She lets them move her, then turn her onto her stomach so that she rests across their two laps, the length of her body fitting easily in the width of the limousine. Her breasts rest against the thigh of one man, her hips over the other. They touch her warmly, safely, through her shirt and skirt. Joanna turns her cheek to the cool leather and closes her eyes.

Fingers are lifting the black fabric of her skirt, easing and folding it up onto the small of her

back, then stroking the smooth silk of her underpants. The other man touches her hair and neck,
and rubs her shoulders. Joanna sighs, already
wet with anticipation, already longing to be
stripped and entered and allowed to moan, but
knowing it is too soon. She feels her underpants
being gathered between fingers and slid down,
uncovering the now healing welts from her
session with the bull-necked man. A wondering
hand traces the cuts, making Joanna shudder
with pleasure.

'Who did this to you?' Rene asks, his voice
curious.

Joanna opens her eyes. 'A man,' she says simply,
and he nods.

'Did you enjoy it?'

'Yes,' Joanna says. 'I had no choice.'

He says nothing, his eyes on her face. The hand is
between her thighs, gently pressing them apart,
stroking the soft skin and the ridges of cuts there.
Joanna wishes it would move farther up to where
she is already moist and open, but the hand seems

content where it is, softly caressing her. 'Please turn over,' she heard Rene say.

Almost lazily, Joanna turns, her arms over her head, the laps of the two men still beneath her shoulders and ass. The hands begin to touch her again, two of them exploring the already tense nipples through her bra and shirt, two of them tenderly playing with her pubic hair, dipping between the lips of her cunt and lightly touching. Joanna moans, arching slightly. The men look down at her without expression. Rene watches from his seat opposite, fascinated. The hands are curious, without urgency. She wants to grab them and push them against her and into her, but they continue to stroke and examine her cunt and covered breasts until it is torturous and she is panting. 'You may sit up,' Rene tells her.

Joanna does. As she rises to settle herself between them again, one of the men calmly gathers her skirt, pulling it to Joanna's waist. The other smoothly draws her underpants over her knees and down, then away. The leather beneath her is already drenched from Joanna's moisture, and slides against her skin, making her seep even more. 'Please spread your legs,' he tells her, and she slowly brings her knees apart, naked and open, her high-heeled shoes resting on the floor of the limousine. As she does, the two men softly lift Joanna's arms and fasten them securely to the back of the seat, at shoulder level, then sit calmly back to await further instructions.

For a long moment, no one speaks. The limousine moves smoothly through the crowded midtown streets, attracting much attention. Each time it stops for a traffic light, pedestrians crowd around, peering intently, trying to see who is inside. Joanna can see from their faces that she is invisible, can see from their easy expressions and curiosity that they cannot tell there is a woman inside, her arms bound apart, her legs spread wide exposing a naked crotch. She loves this sensation of being on display, yet hidden, visible and unseen.

Rene's eyes pass over her face and down her body, lingering at her cunt with a slightly amused expression on his face. He nods at his men and they slowly begin to unbutton Joanna's blouse with delicate fingers, easing it apart, spreading it open, revealing heaving breasts covered with lace. Rene sighs.

'What a lovely bra,' he tells Joanna. 'I'm afraid we will have to cut it off.'

'Of course,' Joanna says.

One of the men removes a switchblade from his pocket. Joanna is completely without fear. He flicks it open and carefully brings it to one of the bra straps, cutting it with a movement of his hand, then he cuts the other. Finally, he snaps apart the lace between her breasts. The other man pulls the bra away, leaving her bare. 'Yes,' Rene says quietly, as if he has just confirmed a private belief. 'Yes.'

The car picks up speed. Joanna closes her eyes. The men on either side of her have begun to touch her breasts with dry, delicate fingers, wonderingly, appreciatively. Rene watches, silent. It is the warmth of his gaze, not the fingers touching her that makes Joanna throb with longing. She imagines the slide of his hips between her spread thighs, the catch of his breath, his long black hair striking the pale skin of her chest as he pounds, hitting her like a feathery whip. A mouth covers her nipple, gently sucking. She thinks of Clarissa, spread-eagled between the wooden posts, shaved and oiled, massaged by anonymous hands, pierced and opened, made to moan. One of the men has moved down, leaving his seat beside her to kneel on the limousine's floor between her knees. She feels his curious fingers glide between the lips of her cunt, parting the hairs. His cheeks softly rub her inner thighs. Joanna arches against him, moaning, and the mouth opens, beginning to lick. She feels suction at the top of her cunt and groans loudly, her eyes snapping open, meeting Rene's eyes. He is smiling fondly at her.

'You are enjoying this,' he says, meaning it as a question.

'Yes,' Joanna whispers, her breath catching.

He considers this as new information. 'And which of my friends would you like to fuck you first?'

She can feel them both tense, listening, their mouths still at her cunt and breast. 'You,' she moans hoarsely. 'I want you.'

As she watches, the smile folds into a grin. The mouths on her body begin again with renewed vigor. The limousine stops for a light and Joanna, glancing briefly out the window, sees bored drivers, passengers nervously checking their watches, crowds of pedestrians hurrying away. 'As you wish,' she hears Rene whisper.

Immediately, the man between her legs moves away, resuming his place beside her, returning to her breast with his moist fingers and insistent mouth. Joanna slides forward on the seat to its edge, arching open, her head back. She hears the rustle of clothing, his jacket removed and carefully folded, then the rough glide of a zipper. Hands come to her sides, new hands, sliding behind her back. Joanna lifts to let him cup her ass, and opens her eyes to see him drawing close. The men move their heads to make room for him, kissing her neck and shoulders, continuing to touch and squeeze her breasts with their hands. Then she is lifted and spread further before being slowly lowered onto him. Joanna gasps as he enters her, sensing his thickness and length. Rene kisses her, giving her his tongue to suck, and Joanna sucks it lovingly, thanking it for her own pleasure. He moves inside her, slowly at first then more urgently. His moan vibrates into her mouth. A hand leaves her breast and travels down to the top of her cunt, where it tangles in the pubic hair and presses, damp and slick. Rene is thrusting deeply into her now, and Joanna moves against him in her own urgency, aware of the three heads covering her own head, the hands caressing her, the pulsing inside her body, the crawl and release of traffic, the growing din of angry cars. 'So sweet,' someone says, breathless. The low, primal yelp of an animal at her ear, Rene gasps into her mouth and Joanna lets herself come to an explosion of horns from outside, releasing the unbearable frustration of a city traffic jam.

Chapter Twenty-One

'I have something a little different for you,' Pauline says on the phone a few days later. Joanna sits cross-legged on her bed.

'Different than what?' She asks, smiling. So far, her experiences with 'O' have *all* been different: from each other and from anything she had ever imagined before.

'Just different,' Pauline says mildly. 'Are you willing?'

'I'm willing to listen,' Joanna says. 'Tell me.'

Pauline sighs into the phone. 'It's an old client of mine. And an old friend, actually, so I've tried to accommodate his needs over the years. He's been seeing the same employee for some time now, but she is getting ready to leave "O" in a few weeks, and I need to find a replacement. Someone who'll be willing to meet regularly with this same client.'

'How often?' Joanna asks.

'Twice a week,' Pauline tells her. 'Tuesdays and Thursdays. In the afternoons.'

'Where?' Joanna wants to know.

'It's an apartment on the west side of the park. Are you interested?'

Joanna considers. She has enjoyed the sporadic nature of her appointments with "O". Until now, she has simply called Pauline whenever she wished, to ask for an assignment. (Pauline has never called her; for obvious reasons, Joanna has not given her telephone number.) Nevertheless, there is something tempting in the idea of a regular appointment. Something solid about it, dependable. If necessary, she thinks, she could even tell Curtis that she is taking a course in the city which meets at those times, a lecture series at a museum, something.

'Yes,' Joanna says finally. 'I'm interested. What does he want?'

Pauline sighs again. 'He is a kind man,' she says carefully. 'Perhaps too kind. He feels he needs punishment for his kindness. He enjoys torture, discipline, helplessness.' She pauses. 'I thought of you, Joanna, because of your experience as an actress. You might find this an invigorating experience, a chance to develop a role. You could still take on other assignments if you like, things more in line with your own needs. But this would have to be regular and reliable. You couldn't cancel the appointment, for example, unless you had an emergency. This man develops a strong relationship with the employee he sees. He's very dependent upon her, emotionally.' She is silent, waiting for Joanna's response. 'I'll tell you what,' Pauline says at last. 'Mr. Banks – that's his name, Mr. Banks – he still has a few more appointments with the woman he's been seeing. Why don't you go and observe one of them, and you can think about it. This Thursday at two?' She recites an address and Joanna writes it down. 'You can go and then let me know,' Pauline says. 'Arrive a bit early, and I'll tell Rochelle to expect you. She can answer your questions.'

'All right,' Joanna says. 'But it doesn't really sound like something I'd like. Frankly, it sounds a little strange.'

'Perhaps,' Pauline says absently. 'But then, perhaps someone else might call your own desires strange.'

'Probably,' Joanna admits, blushing. 'I'll go, don't worry.'

'Good,' says Pauline. 'I hoped you would. This man,' she says, 'remember, he's a good man. Also, he's extremely rich. He's been generous to the women he's seen before.'

'That doesn't matter,' Joanna tells her. 'I mean, that's not why I work for "O".'

Pauline says nothing.

'Goodbye,' Joanna says, but as she says it she suddenly hears a low buzz from the telephone, and knows that Pauline has already hung up.

Chapter Twenty-Two

Joanna takes a taxi from the train station through an overcast afternoon. She carries but does not wear her black bracelet, unsure of whether it will be required. She is here to watch, she reminds herself. Just to watch. She is already convinced, however, that this – whatever 'this' turns out to be – is not for her. She loathes the idea of humiliating someone else, despite the fact that she has so enjoyed her own various humiliations through 'O'. She will simply watch and learn, and then she will call Pauline and say that no, she's sorry, she wouldn't be any good at this.

The taxi lets her off in front of a brownstone, a few blocks west of the park. The trees along the street move softly in the wet breeze. Joanna pays the driver then climbs the steps to the front door. When her ring is answered, she pushes the heavy door and climbs to the apartment.

Rochelle waits in the open door, tall and smiling. She has dark hair, cut marine-short in an almost Punk style that suits her long neck and strong features. She reaches forward, extending her hand as Joanna climbs the last steps, and Joanna shakes it. 'I'm Rochelle,' she says. 'It's good to meet you, Joanna.'

'Thanks,' Joanna says. 'Thanks for letting me watch.'

'No problem,' Rochelle says, pulling the door open. 'Come on in.'

Joanna walks into a small room, almost bare except for a short bureau of drawers, a standing mirror, a few chairs. It looks so normal, she is thinking, wondering how any convincing act of humiliation could possibly take place in such an unthreatening space. Rochelle, watching her face, laughs softly. 'Back in there,' she says, beckoning. 'He changes in this room.'

Joanna follows. The apartment is formed in the old-fashioned Railroad manner, one room behind another, each opening into the one behind it. The room into which they now pass is long, painted grey, carpeted in black and dimly lit. Whips are mounted on the walls, an astonishing variety of lengths and thicknesses. Chains hang down in pairs, heavy and black, with large manacles attached. Joanna takes in a curious black chair with leather straps, a low table with adjustable panels, more mirrors, a black, vaguely medical chest with silver handles on its drawers. Another set of chains hangs down from the ceiling. 'Jesus,' she says softly, surprising herself by saying it out loud.

Rochelle chuckles in front of her. 'I know what you mean. The first time I saw it I nearly died.' They enter the third and final room, another small bedroom with a closet, chest of drawers, an adjacent bathroom.

'Who owns this apartment?' Joanna asks. "'O"?'

'No,' Rochelle shakes her head. 'The man owns it, Mr. Banks. He bought it for his appointments, and we designed it according to his specifications. He was very particular about what he wanted.' Joanna sits in an armchair by the rear window. Rochelle unself-consciously begins to change into a black leather bustier, black leather pants studded with silver, heavy black boots, high heeled.

'How long have you been doing this?' Joanna asks.

'About two years. I'd still be doing it, but I'm getting married next month and we're moving out of the city.'

Joanna leans forward. 'Does your fiancé know about "O"?' She asks.

Rochelle looks up and smiles. 'You could say,' she laughs, 'that we met on the job.'

Joanna laughs too. Rochelle fastens a black bracelet on her wrist. Automatically, Joanna reaches into her bag to find her own.

'You don't have to,' Rochelle says. 'He won't be able to see us. He wears a black hood with an opening at the mouth. I just wear mine out of nostalgia. I'll have to give it back to Pauline soon.'

They hear the rasp of a key and the front door swings open. Joanna stiffens.

'We still have a few minutes,' Rochelle says. 'He changes in the front room then waits for me in the chamber. He puts on his own hood and usually underpants, and stands facing the wall until I tell him what to do.'

'What do you have to wear?' Joanna asks.

Rochelle shrugs. 'I can really wear anything,' she says. 'I mean, he doesn't see me. But he likes the feel of the leather against his skin, so I wear that. Also,' she smiles, 'I find it helps me get into the proper mood.' She pauses. 'Pauline says you're an actress.'

'Yes,' Joanna nods.

'That's good. Just pretend you're full of rage at him, you're going to punish him. He likes pain, but he needs to believe that you really mean to hurt him, you know, push him beyond the point where it isn't pleasurable anymore. He needs to feel the threat before he can enjoy it. Make him grovel. Make him please you. Do anything you want to him, but always make sure you end the session at four o'clock exactly. Just untie him if he's tied up, and come back here. Then wait for him to leave.'

'You mean,' Joanna asks, confused, 'you never see him except in that room?'

'Right,' Rochelle nods. 'That's how he wants it.' Then, taking in Joanna's perplexity, she smiles. 'Don't worry, Joanna. You're going to be good at this. I know it.'

Joanna shakes her head. 'Actually,' she says, 'I'm pretty sure I'm not going to take the assignment. It really doesn't sound like my thing, to tell you the truth.'

Rochelle sighs. 'Well, you'll have a look. We can talk again afterwards,' she says as they both hear the man enter the chamber next door. There is a shuffle, then silence. Rochelle gets to her feet. 'Now,' she says, 'he'll know that you're here, that he's being watched. I won't introduce you, of course. We don't use names. He calls me "Mistress", okay?'

'Okay,' Joanna says. 'I'm ready.'

Rochelle opens the door and Joanna follows her into the chamber. Dimly, at the far end of the room, she can make out a figure, black hooded and wearing what look like women's black silk underpants, standing in the corner, facing into it. Joanna finds a seat on a low leather stool and tries to make herself comfortable. Rochelle steps up to him and stops, letting him feel her presence, and he visibly trembles. 'We have a guest today,' she says, her voice cruel at his ear. 'My friend has come to watch you, to see how bad you are and why I am forced to punish you. She is watching you carefully,' Rochelle tells him, reaching up to remove a long whip from the wall, and casually flicking it in the air. Joanna hears a sharp intake of breath, muffled by the leather hood. 'So you'd better be good,' Rochelle breathes, continuing, 'or I'll have to hurt you and make you scream. Do you understand?'

The hooded head nods, resigned.

'Then turn around,' she says.

The body turns, slowly. Rochelle cracks the whip. Joanna gasps, glad that the man is blinded, glad that Rochelle faces away from her because she is pale and damp and shaking. This groveling captive, clad in leather and silk panties, bending willingly for the whip with an ecstatic sigh, is Curtis.

PART THREE

A Question of Control

Chapter Twenty-Three

She makes him kneel, and crawl across the carpet. Joanna hears him whimper inside the leather mask. Rochelle tells him to shut up, Does he want to be whipped? No, moans the voice, at once intimately familiar to Joanna and strangely foreign. She whips him anyway, a light touch to the backs of his thighs, and Joanna flinches as if she herself had been struck. Rochelle tells him to stop where he is, on all fours, then calmly sits on his ass, her legs crossed, and smokes a cigarette, flicking the ash over his back. Her other hand rests on his buttocks, patting them now and then. She asks him questions. Has he been good? Is he going to do what she tells him to do, exactly what she says? How severely will he need to be punished? Curtis answers in a low voice, racked with fear. When he gives an answer Rochelle doesn't like, she reaches between his legs, pinching his testicles through the black silk, and Curtis groans.

Joanna watches, numb. The groveling, black-hooded man before her, while undeniably her own husband, is unlike any man she has ever known. Visibly aroused by his humiliation, alert to the shift of weight on his back, the filaments of heat stinging his skin as the cigarette ash is sprinkled there, utterly in thrall to the voice that insults him. She thinks of herself on Curtis's lap, his hand comforting on her thigh, his fond breath in her gossamer hair. She thinks of his 'phase', as he put it, the separate bedrooms, the frequent reassurances that she is beautiful, lovely, that he loves the idea of her waiting for him at home, reading her book, being his sweet young wife, his generous offer of support if she ever feels the need to do volunteer work . . .

And then, without warning, Joanna feels her entire body flood with rage, shake with it. The lowered head moans with pleasure as his testicles are grasped and twisted. She wants, suddenly, to give him real pain, pain far beyond pleasure, pain beyond anything she can imagine for herself. All of the affection she has ever felt for Curtis leaves her in a rush, irrevocably, and is replaced by a hatred more pure and towering than she thought possible. She would like to destroy him.

Rochelle rises, making him follow her like a dog crawling behind, his hooded face raised to her ass. She leads him back to the wall, calls him 'you dumb shit', tells him to get to his feet and raise his arms. He does. She fastens them to the manacles hanging from the wall, yanking each one harshly when it snaps. Curtis give a groan of pain and she tells him to shut the fuck up. Rochelle stands behind him and presses herself against him, letting him feel the pointed impressions of her breasts against his skin, through the leather. Curtis' breath quickens. Then, abruptly, she steps back and rips at his underpants, pulling them down to mid-thigh, telling him to spread his legs for her, that's right, spread them farther, giving Joanna a view of her husband she has never had before, open and exposed, his balls tight with arousal, his cock jerking wetly in front. Rochelle's hand fondles him briefly, then she gently brings a riding crop between his legs, letting it trawl up and down each thigh, then using it to lift his cock and lower it. Curtis sighs, the sound of a whistle against the black leather. 'You want it, don't you?' Rochelle croons, drawing the crop through the crack of Curtis' ass, letting the tip pause at his anus. 'Don't you, you worthless cunt?'

'Yes,' Curtis moans. 'Yes, Mistress.'

'All right then,' she says. 'I'll give it to you.'

Joanna watches, open-mouthed, as Rochelle whips him, bringing the crop down on his buttocks, his thighs, his tensed calves. She watches the welts rise along his skin, new welts among the scars of many past ones. Joanna wonders how she could never have seen them before, not even by chance as he was dressing or bathing, but then Curtis dresses alone in his room and bathes with the door locked, emerging from the bathroom dressed for bed in his pyjamas and robe. One of the cuts on his ass has opened and begun, slowly, to bleed, Rochelle pauses in her frenzy and takes the drop of blood on her finger, then pushes it into the leather hole where his mouth is visible. 'Suck that,' she hisses, and he does, making sounds. She yanks her finger from his mouth and lowers it along Curtis's chest, lightly touching the nipple, then fiercely pinching it. He groans, and Rochelle laughs softly. 'Now you know,' she says, her voice intimate, 'you know we're not alone today, don't you?'

'Yes,' Curtis says.

'And you know how bad you've been,' she croons.

'Yes, Mistress.'

'So I've asked my friend to help me,' Rochelle says. 'Because she's had experience with bad boys who need to be punished, and she knows how to give them pain, to make them good. Obviously, I've been too easy on you, because I see how bad you are. And so you're going to lie down on the table and spread your legs for her, and she is going to punish you the way you deserve to be punished, and if you scream she will only give you more pain. Do you understand?'

'Yes, Mistress,' says Joanna's husband.

Rochelle unsnaps his manacles and turns him around, leading him to the low bench, then pushing him forward. Curtis sprawls, his chest against the leather. Rochelle attaches rubber manacles to his wrists and fastens them together, behind his back. The end of the bench is beneath Curtis's hips. Rochelle kneels behind him and forces his legs wide apart, then pauses to thoughtfully fondle his cock, which dangles over the edge. Then she turns to Joanna and extends the whip. 'Are you ready, my dear?' She asks, smiling.

Joanna knows that she doesn't have to do it. Rochelle can simply walk to her corner and back again, then beat him herself. She looks at the pale skin of her husband against the black leather, the wide V of his legs, the dangling genitals and dark anal open-ing surrounded by gray hairs. Curtis moans deeply inside the leather mask. Joanna gets to her feet.

'Yes,' she says in a voice that is low and hoarse and foreign, even to her. 'I'm ready.' Rochelle places the whip in her hand.

Chapter Twenty-Four

'You'll never guess what happened to me today,' Joanna says over dinner. Curtis passes her the salad bowl and she helps herself. 'I had the strangest adventure.'

'What?' her husband asks. 'Tell me.'

'I went to the city,' Joanna says. 'I don't know why. I suppose I was just bored, and I got it in my head to visit a museum. So I got dressed and took the train in.'

'How nice,' Curtis says, sipping his wine. 'How nice for you to have a change.'

'Well,' says Joanna, 'I went to the art museum near the park, and I walked around there for a while. And while I was sitting in the Impressionist gallery, this very nice woman came and sat next to me, and we started talking. She's an artist.'

'Really!' Curtis says, cutting his lamb chop.

'Yes. Well, anyway, we started talking about art. And it turns out that she studies at this place called the . . . um . . . Art Student something.'

'Art Student's Institute,' Curtis says knowingly. Joanna smiles in gratitude.

'Yes, that's it. The Art Student's Institute. They have classes, you know, and the teacher comes and talks to you about your painting, and everyone paints the same thing like a bowl of fruit. And it sounded wonderful and I just thought, this is what I need!'

'Hm,' says Curtis.

'So,' Joanna continues, 'I went right over there and signed up for a class!'

Curtis puts down his fork. 'You did?'

'Yes,' Joanna nods excitedly. 'Tuesdays and Thursdays, in the afternoon. I've already bought a sketchpad and some paints. I can't wait to begin!' Curtis is silent, watching her. 'You know, I've been spending so many afternoons at the beach lately, and it's been nice. But I got to thinking how much fun it would be to be able to paint. Then I could drive around and make pictures. Wouldn't you like that?'

'Of course,' Curtis says, smiling fondly at her. 'It's just that the Art Student's Institute often has classes with nude models. I don't think I really like the idea of you drawing some naked man. Frankly, I don't think it's proper.'

'Oh *no*!' Joanna gasps. 'I wouldn't do that.' She giggles. 'I'm not very interested in naked men. But I thought it would be nice if I could learn to do land-scapes. Then I could sit here on the porch and draw the ocean. Wouldn't that be nice?'

He relaxes into his smile. Joanna has, after all, simply refined his own vision of her, waiting for him on the porch, occupying herself till he comes home. She knows that he will now embrace the idea.

'Of course,' Curtis says. 'How lovely.'

After dinner, he brings her art books from his library upstairs, spreading them open on the coffee table and pointing things out for her, humoring her newfound interest. Joanna struggles to look interested, to nod, to praise and admire his expertise. She can't wait until he says he is ready for bed, so that she herself can go to bed. The sooner she falls asleep, Joanna thinks, the sooner she will wake up, and the sooner she can telephone Pauline to say that she will accept the assignment.

Chapter Twenty-Five

'I thought you might,' Pauline says simply, then pauses. 'I mean,' she adds, 'because you were an actress. I thought it might appeal to you.'

'It does,' Joanna says. 'I might even enjoy it.'

'Good,' Pauline says. 'You know, Joanna, an important part of what I do is the matching up of clients and employees. Which combinations of people will provide the most pleasure for all concerned.' She laughs. 'I've made marriages, you know. I expect Rochelle told you how she met her fiancé.'

'Yes,' Joanna says.

'Sometimes, to be honest, people are surprised. Their horizons are broadened. They discover talents they didn't know they had, desires they didn't know they had, and then when those desires are satisfied, the pleasure is intensified.' She pauses. 'Take yourself for example.'

'What?' Joanna says.

'Your initial experience with anal penetration was unpleasant, wasn't it? Or so you told Mr. Stephens. And yet several of the men you've seen since have reported your taking some pleasure in it. Is that true?'

'Yes,' Joanna says, blushing. She prefers not to think about the intimacies exchanged by Pauline and her clients. There will be no privacy, she recalls being told by Mr. Stephens.

'Well, in any case, I'm pleased,' Pauline is saying. 'I sensed an aptitude for this kind of work. I thought you might rise to the challenge.'

'I will,' Joanna says. 'I'll try.'

Pauline gives her instructions, confirming times and dates. A key to the apartment will be left for her with Pauline's doorman. The rear bedroom of the apartment is full of appropriate clothing – she should wear whatever fits, whatever feels right. If she has questions, if she wants anything, if there is equipment that needs to be replaced, she should get in touch. If she wants to take on other work, she should get in touch. 'But do call me anyway,' Pauline says. 'Just to keep in touch, to check in now and then. It's always a pleasure to talk to you, Joanna.'

'Thank you,' she says.

'And you'll keep in touch?'

'Of course.'

'All right then, good luck. Joanna? I think you will enjoy this job.'

Joanna hangs up the phone. 'I think you're right,' she says to the empty room.

Chapter Twenty-Six

Arriving early at the apartment, Joanna explores the chamber. She tests the straps on the low table and chair, and practices snapping and unsnapping the manacles. Each whip is lifted and examined, tentatively flicked in the air so that she can learn its sounds and weight and potential pain. The drawers in the black bureau are full of interesting things: lubricant, studded collars, curious leather pieces meant, she supposes, to be tightened around genitals, an astonishing array of rubber phalluses.

In the rear bedroom, Joanna finds an ample collection of clothing, and chooses for herself a black bustier like Rochelle's but with garters attached, black stockings, heavy boots. She fits a black wig over her own gossamer hair, not because she is afraid that Curtis will see her but because she wants to create a new physical self for the new bitterness seething within her. Red lipstick, dark eye shadow, drops of musk essence beneath her arms and between her breasts. Joanna, considering herself in the mirror, sees a breathtaking stranger, hardened and cruel and ready to inflict severe pain. She smiles at this new woman, liking her, wanting to know her better.

The front door clicks. Joanna sits on the bed, listening, readying herself. She hears the familiar sounds of Curtis undressing, a comfortable groan as he stretches. The door to the chamber opens and shuts. Joanna listens to the sound of his tread over the carpet, then the crackle of stiff leather, a hood coming down over his head. Joanna breathes deeply, steadying herself. When she is ready, she walks to the chamber door, and enters.

Curtis stands facing the wall, his hooded head bowed forward, his hands at his sides. Joanna paces behind him, letting him listen for a moment, letting him feel the newness of the tread, the slight unfamiliarity. 'Turn around,' she says at last, in the strained and husky voice she had been practicing for days. 'Your back against the wall.'

She walks towards him and raises his arms over his head, snapping them into the manacles. Her fingers tremble slightly when they touch his skin, but Curtis is lost in his own trembling, and does not seem to notice. When he is locked into place, Joanna lets herself touch him, a finger sliding down his stomach and lightly over his cock, making it harden inside the silk underpants. She steps back and finds a seat, a few feet away from him.

'I am your Mistress,' Joanna says softly but firmly. 'I want you to understand that I consider you my property and my slave. You are here to please me and for no other reason. Do you understand?'

'Yes, Mistress,' her husband says.

'If you please me,' Joanna continues, 'I will reward you with pleasure. But if you displease me, I will punish you with pain, more pain than you can imagine. Do you understand?'

'Yes, Mistress,' he whimpers.

'I will do exactly as I wish with you. Whatever you do beyond the walls of this room, whatever status you have, is worthless to me. To me, you are nothing. Less than nothing. Here you exist only to give me pleasure. Your worth is entirely dependent upon that, and nothing else. I will learn what you can bear, and what you cannot bear. Your life is in my hands. Do you understand?'

'Yes, Mistress,' Curtis moans.

She stands and without warning reaches between his legs, squeezing the stiffness of his cock through the silk. 'Why are you hard?' Joanna demands. 'Did I tell you to be hard?'

'No, Mistress,' says Curtis.

'Get rid of it,' she hisses, leaning close. He moans. His cock pulses in her hand. 'Get rid of it immediately,' she tells him, 'or I will be forced to punish you.'

Joanna steps back and watches carefully, seeing the beginning of perspiration over his chest. The bulge between his legs only grows. She shakes her head.

'I see we are not off to a good start,' Joanna says, resigned. 'I had hoped you would at least try to obey me.'

'Please,' Curtis groans. 'Please, I can't help it.'

She reaches for a whip. 'Bullshit,' she says softly. 'You're not trying.'

'Please,' he says again. 'Don't hurt me.'

'Be quiet,' Joanna says. 'Don't make me punish you for impudence as well.' Lightly, she taps the end of the whip against the bulge.

'God,' Curtis moans. Joanna cracks the whip loudly in the air. He flinches.

'*I* am your God!' She shouts. 'No one else can help you here.'

'Yes, Mistress,' he mutters, his chest heaving.

Joanna steps close to him and rips at his underpants, pulling them down to his knees. Then she kneels at his feet to examine him, letting her breath ruffle the grey hairs at his crotch. A drop of semen glistens at the tip of his straining cock. Joanna considers.

Crossing the room, she lubricates her finger, then returns, telling him to spread his legs. Curtis does, as far as the underpants stretched between his knees allow. Then, without preparing him, she deftly pushes her finger into his rectum.

Curtis moans with undisguised pleasure. His cock jerks in Joanna's face.

Her mouth drops open in shock. She is astonished by his reaction, had meant to cause him pain. Then her astonishment turns to rage, that she has pleased him, that he dares to be pleased in this way. She jerks her finger away and detaches Curtis's wrists, grabbing them and pulling him forward into the center of the room. There, she hooks him again overhead, his hands together, snapped into the manacles which dangle from the ceiling, then tightening the chain until he is stretched to his full length. Joanna inserts her boot between his knees and calmly steps, pushing the silk underpants to the floor, letting him feel the leather. She hears his sigh as he is stripped.

Carefully, Joanna studies him, the sheen of sweat over his chest, the wet and open lips visible through the hole in his hood, the engorged cock sticking out at a right angle from his body. The cock, especially, enrages her. Joanna goes to the bureau and removes one of the leather bonds she had examined earlier, this one with pointed silver studs protruding from it. Smiling, she fastens it about his waist and legs, then slowly tightens the silver studs around his erection, letting the metal rub into his skin. Curtis moans with pain.

'Good,' Joanna says. 'Remember this. Your cock is at my disposal. You're hard when I want you to be hard, and only then. If you disobey me, you will wear this to remind you.'

'Yes, Mistress,' Curtis says.

She stands back and lets the whip drift over his body, avoiding his groin. It glides through the hair beneath his arms, over the skin of his neck, across his chest. Then she pokes the tip through the hole in his hood and tells him to suck it. 'Pretend,' she whispers, close to his face, 'that this is my breast. Show me how you would like to suck me. Think of my nipple in your mouth, hard and pointed. Show me what you would like to do to it.' Curtis sucks, his mouth greedy. Joanna yanks the whip away and turns him at the hips. 'You *wish*,' she sneers. 'Don't you just *wish*. But you haven't earned it yet, have you?'

'No, Mistress,' he whimpers, hanging his head.

'Not by a long shot,' she confirms. 'And now I have to punish you, don't I?'

'Yes,' she hears him say.

'And how do I punish you?' Joanna asks her husband.

'With the whip.'

'And where do I whip you?'

'Everywhere,' he moans. 'I deserve to be whipped.'

'All right,' she says, obliging him.

The whip lands squarely across his ass. Joanna loves the moment of contact, the sound of smacking, the miraculous red lines that appear out of nowhere. Over and over she lets it fall, breaking the skin. Curtis yelps in pain and she loves that too. Then the tender insides of his thighs. She would like to get him on his back, she thinks, and make him spread his legs in the air, then let it fall between his open legs. Abandoning the whip, she begins to slap him with her hands, feeling the buttocks ripple as she makes contact, flushed with heat, then softly caressing the skin she has just punished. Curtis moans, his hips moving slightly, lightly thrusting into the cruel studs. 'All right,' Joanna says softly. 'I'll tell you what we're going to do.'

She unfastens his wrists and they fall limply to his sides. She takes his left hand between her palms and rubs it, twisting the gold wedding ring between her fingers. 'What is this?' She asks.

He stammers, confused. 'A ring. I'm married.'

'Oh,' Joanna breathes. 'Married. Tell me,' she whispers, unbuckling the straps around his groin, pulling them away, 'do you fuck your wife?'

He pauses. 'Yes, Mistress.'

'Good,' Joanna says. 'Then show me. Show me how you get yourself hard for your wife.' She smears lubricant across his palm and brings it to his cock. 'Show me,' Joanna whispers. Slowly, he begins to touch himself, taking himself in his hand and rubbing it from root to tip. The cock recovers from its contact with the metal studs, lengthening, stiffening. 'Good,' Joanna croons. 'I want you hard, as hard as you can get. But don't come, I'm warning you. If you come, I will give you unbearable pain. Do you understand?'

'Yes,' he gasps, visibly aroused by her threat. She steps back to watch him masturbate, luxuriating in his moans, his frustration, his fear of coming.

'Listen to me,' Joanna says quietly. 'Before I see you again you will fuck your wife and make her come. You will remember everything about it, the way she smells, the way she tastes. And when you come back here, you will tell me what you did. You will leave nothing out. Do you understand?'

'Yes,' Curtis moans.

'Let go of yourself,' she says, her strange voice ringing huskily in her ears. Immediately, he stops. Joanna steps up close to him, close enough for her breasts to brush against his chest. Reaching down, she calmly fingers his pubic hair, and watches his mouth open in longing. 'Don't move,' she tells him. 'Don't move, and, above all, don't come. Do you understand?'

'Yes,' he says, his voice barely audible.

Joanna kneels at her husband's feet. With the tip of her tongue, she collects the drop of semen from the end of his cock and noisily tastes it. Curtis trembles, holding himself back. She opens her mouth and washes the underside of his cock with her tongue, lightly stroking his scrotum with her fingers. 'Don't,' he cries, and immediately she brings the flat of her hand up between his legs in a smack, making him jerk in pain. Before he can recover, she takes him deep into her mouth, sucking him lovingly. His stiffness over her tongue fills her suddenly with regret, a whiff of the affection she once felt for him. I would have done this for you,

Joanna thinks as she sucks her husband. I would have done this, if you'd asked.

Curtis moans, involuntarily making small thrusts into her mouth. Then, without warning, he comes, gasping in horror. Joanna clamps her teeth in rage. Getting roughly to her feet, she pushes him down, his head to the floor, chest folded against his knees, whimpering in terror. She stands over him, his head pinned between her ankles. 'Get ready,' she whispers fiercely, taking up her whip. She smiles at the quivering crack of his ass. 'Get ready,' Joanna tells him, seething. 'Here it comes.'

Chapter Twenty-Seven

'Tell me about your wife,' she asks him the following week. 'Did you do what I commanded you to do?'

'Yes,' Curtis says. 'Yes, Mistress.'

She has him face-down on the table, his wrists bound behind his back, his legs braced apart on the floor, stretched open to her from behind.

Joanna knows he is lying. At home, Curtis has behaved entirely as he has always behaved towards her: tender, admiring, chaste.

'Tell me,' she says, standing over him, letting the end of her riding crop brush the backs of his thighs.

'I . . .' He begins, awkwardly. 'She was on the bed.'

'Oh, good,' Joanna croons. Then, cruelly, 'Where else would she be?'

'I kissed her. I . . . touched her breast.'

'Tell me about her breasts.'

Curtis sighs. Joanna notices the gradual softening of his cock. So that is what he thinks of me, she sighs. That's how much I excite him.

'Firm,' he is stammering, 'and . . . um . . . not very large.'

'Her nipples,' Joanna moans, gliding the crop over his scrotum.

'Tight,' Curtis whispers. 'Hard and tight. Pink. Wet.'

'And you sucked them,' she prompts, wetting her finger and drawing it through the crack of his ass.

'Yes,' he says, breathless.

Joanna kneels by the table, near his head. Reaching into her bustier she pulls the leather from her breast. The nipple is hard. She pushes it into the hole where his mouth is visible. 'Show me,' she tells him. 'Show me how you suck your wife.'

He sucks, his mouth hungry. If only you had, she thinks, holding his head against her. If only you were telling the truth. She pushes him away.

'What else? Tell me about her cunt.'

'Wet,' he says. 'Warm, sweet. I licked her.'

'Oh!' Joanna says, delighted with this new information and its attendant possibilities. Walking to Curtis' head, she straddles the narrow table and pushes her crotch against the top of his leather hood. 'Show me,' she says. 'Lick my cunt.'

He lifts his head and begins to lick her, letting his tongue glide deep inside, lapping at the edges of her crotch, moaning with pleasure.

Joanna, despite herself, moans too, thrusting slightly against him, wishing more of his mouth were accessible through the leather hood. Almost, she lets herself come, but bitterness overwhelms her arousal and she pulls away from him. Taking a phallus from the bureau drawer, she smears it with lubricant and steps behind him.

'Then you fucked her,' Joanna says. 'Didn't you?'

'Yes,' Curtis says. Joanna reaches between his legs and starts to massage him.

'First you got hard for her, so hard you thought you were bursting. Didn't you?' Her fingers run over the slippery tip and he groans.

'Yes, I was hard.'

Joanna presses the rubber phallus against his sphincter. 'And you entered her. Didn't you?'

'Yes,' Curtis says, and as he does, Joanna nudges the phallus inside. He groans loudly.

'Then you pushed,' she croons, pushing steadily. 'Didn't you?'

'Yes,' he cries. 'Oh, yes, I did.'

'And when it was all the way inside, then what did you do?'

'I pulled it out,' Curtis gasps. Joanna withdraws the phallus. 'Then I pushed it again.' She obliges him and he sighs deeply.

'How did you fuck her?' Joanna asks, caressing him. 'Fast and rhythmic? Or slow and deep?'

'Slow,' he manages, breathless. 'Deep.'

Accordingly, Joanna fucks him, watching his cock throb with pleasure, the gathering and build of his climax, his thrusts, backwards against the fullness in his rectum. 'Oh,' he moans, about to come, 'Oh, yes . . .'

Quietly, Joanna's hand drops from his cock. The phallus is still inside him. She gets softly to her feet.

Curtis, aware of what is happening, whimpers in frustration. Joanna takes a long whip from the wall.

'You know,' she says thoughtfully, swishing it through the air, 'there's something about your story I don't quite believe.'

'Mistress . . .' Curtis groans.

'I can't quite put my finger on it,' she continues, ignoring him. 'Something about your description of your wife doesn't quite ring true. I think,' she says, decisively, 'I think you may be lying to me.'

'Oh no,' he cries. 'Oh God, no, I'm not lying.'

'But I think you are,' Joanna says fiercely. 'You're lying to me. You didn't fuck your wife at all.'

'I did!' Like a child, Joanna thinks, smirking. A child saying, 'I did too!'

'No!' She snaps the whip in the air over his head and he shudders. 'You're lying, you worthless piece of shit. And now you're going to pay. Aren't you?'

'Yes,' he moans, resigned. 'Yes, Mistress.'

She steps behind him, letting the whip tap his buttocks around the protruding stump of the phallus. 'And you deserve to be punished, don't you?'

'Yes. I deserve it, Mistress.'

She starts to beat him, loving his pain. 'I agree,' she tells him, meaning it.

Chapter Twenty-Eight

'How are the art lessons coming?' he asks that night over dinner. 'You've had a few by now, haven't you?'

'Yes,' Joanna nods, letting him scoop a second helping of steamed vegetables onto her plate. 'I'm enjoying them. I find that I'm even better at it than I thought I might be.'

'Good,' he nods, fondly. 'Tell me about it.'

Joanna smiles. 'The teacher is a woman, really beautiful but sort of hard, you know? She has black hair, about to her shoulders, and she always wears these leather pants. Really kind of butch,' she laughs. 'But she says I'm good. We've been doing this still life, with a whole bunch of things on the table.'

'Like what?' Asks Curtis, a little absently.

'Oh,' Joanna considers. 'Fruit, of course. I mean, I guess you sort of have to have fruit, right? And there's a rubber ball, and a tube of paint and a coffee can. And there's a whip.'

Curtis puts down his fork. 'A whip?' He asks, puzzled.

'Yes,' Joanna says, shrugging. 'Don't ask me.'

'What kind of whip,' he presses.

'Oh, I don't know,' she smiles. 'I mean, I'm not too familiar with whips, you know. It's sort of long and black.' She pauses. 'I guess it's maybe the kind you would use on a horse.'

'A riding crop,' he nods authoritatively. Joanna suppresses a smile.

'I guess.'

He eats silently for a moment. 'I'd love to see some of what you've been doing,' he tells her, and she blushes.

'Oh, not yet! I don't have anything good enough yet. I want you to be proud of me.'

'Honey,' Curtis says gently. 'I am. I am proud of you. I love you.' He lifts her hand and kisses it tenderly. Joanna's lips purse in distaste.

Rising, Curtis opens the refrigerator to put away the wine. Joanna senses the stiffness of his gait beneath his trousers. Remembering the beating she gave him only hours before, she isn't surprised.

'Sweetheart,' she says, concerned, 'are you limping?'

He turns to her. 'Maybe a bit,' Curtis says carefully. 'Stupid of me, I tripped today in the hall. Right outside my office. Very embarrassing. I'm fine, though.'

'But darling!' she cries. 'How awful! You'll have to get into a bath right away. You poor thing.' Joanna rises and walks around the table to him, laying a hand on his thigh. He winces slightly. 'Where does it hurt?' She asks, feeling. 'Would you like me to give you a massage? I can make it feel better.'

'Oh no,' he says smoothly, backing away. 'It isn't bad. But perhaps you're right about the bath. In fact, I think I'll just go and start running it now.'

'All right,' Joanna says, looking disappointed. 'Are you sure about the massage? I'm happy to do it. I hate to see you in pain.'

Curtis smiles and reaches for her, taking her gently in his arms and nuzzling her hair. 'You're an angel,' he murmurs. 'A sweet angel. I love you for worrying about me, but you needn't. See you later.'

'All right, sweetheart,' she whispers, watching him turn and leave the kitchen. She loathes him.

Chapter Twenty-Nine

'Ah, Joanna,' Pauline says when Joanna telephones a few days later, 'I've been wanting to speak with you.'

'Is everything all right?' Joanna asks.

'Of course!' Pauline laughs. 'You're doing beautifully, if that's what you mean. Two of the clients you saw before Mr. Banks are desperate to see you again.'

'Which ones?' Joanna says, mildly curious, but Pauline only chuckles.

'Does it matter? No, I want to speak with you about something else. In fact, I'd like to talk in person if it's all right with you. Why don't you come to tea. Tomorrow? Are you free tomorrow?'

'Yes,' Joanna says. She is not due to see Curtis again until the following day.

'About two o'clock, then,' Pauline tells her happily. 'See you then.'

Joanna is surprised to find that this conversation leaves her with no pleasure, no satisfaction. Instead, she is vaguely disturbed by it, and troubled with a strange sense of foreboding. Indeed, by the following afternoon when she presents herself to Pauline's uniformed doorman, Joanna has convinced herself that she is about to be offered another Curtis, perhaps a series of Curtises, as a subspecialty of some sort. Probably, she thinks, he has raved to his first wife about Joanna's ferocity, the murderous intensity of the pain and pleasure she causes him, and now Pauline has been inspired to service other clients with similar needs.

She will just say no, Joanna decides. After all, that is her right as an employee of 'O', to say no.

Pauline is all smiles as she opens the door to her

penthouse, answering Joanna's knock. She ushers Joanna inside saying 'Welcome, welcome,' and 'You look lovely this afternoon, Joanna.'

Joanna thanks her and walks behind Pauline into a large, beautifully furnished living room. There is a stunning Persian rug before the hearth and a large Impressionist oil over the mantelpiece, which Joanna vaguely recognizes. Beneath a wall of high windows, the park stretches, lush and green.

'Now,' Pauline says when they are settled on a pair of luxurious matching sofas, 'how do you take your tea?'

She is pouring into delicate china from an elaborate silver teapot. Joanna asks for sugar and lemon. She accepts a small sandwich from the plate Pauline passes to her.

'Tell me Joanna,' Pauline says, sipping her tea, 'how are you getting on with our friend on the west side?'

'Well enough,' she answers carefully. 'He's a strange sort of man. I pity him, actually.'

Pauline nods. 'So do I, to be frank. But he is, as I told you, an old friend. I try to give him what he needs.'

'Yes,' says Joanna, 'but how did he get that way?'

'Who knows?' She shrugs. 'How does anyone get the way they are? Why should any of us be pleased by one thing and disgusted by the next? In this business,' Pauline smiles, 'I've learned not to judge.'

'I hope you're not thinking of sending me to another client like that,' Joanna says warily. 'I mean, with similar needs.'

Pauline laughs. 'Oh no, Joanna. Absolutely not. There's only one Curtis. I think we both realize that, don't we?'

Slowly, Joanna lets the awareness sink in. Pauline has used Curtis's real name, kindly, intimately. A quick glance at her face reveals that she knows everything, and Joanna gasps and covers her mouth with her hand. Pauline reaches across to kindly pat Joanna's knee. 'Don't worry,' she says.

Joanna sinks back into the cushions. 'I asked Mr. Stephens not to tell,' Joanna says, feeling on the point of tears.

'You asked him not to tell Curtis,' Pauline says. 'And he didn't. He told me. But perhaps,' she says softly, 'I already knew.'

Joanna sits up abruptly. 'Did you?'

'Perhaps,' she says. 'Does it matter? I know now.'

'Yes,' Joanna sighs, resigned. 'Well, I suppose that's it. I'll quit, of course. I mean,' she adds formally, 'I'm willing to terminate my employment, if you'll just promise not to tell him.'

'But why?' Pauline cries. 'Why would I ever ask you to do such a thing? I wouldn't dream of denying my clients the pleasure of your company. Not to mention your own pleasure, Joanna.' She laughs softly. 'Not to mention Curtis's. I think he would be devastated to lose such an enthusiastic mistress.'

'Then what?' Joanna says flatly. 'Why did you ask me here?'

'It's very simple,' she says. 'There's someone here I want you to meet. Someone who wants very much to meet you.'

'A client?' Joanna asks, her voice dull. Pauline shakes her head.

'Not a client. It's my son. Mine and Curtis's. Would you like to meet him?'

Joanna looks around the room. Dimly, beyond it, she becomes aware of sounds in another part of the apartment. Someone else is here.

'No,' she says, alarmed. Joanna gets to her feet and reaches down for her bag. 'I don't want to meet him. I want to leave.'

'But it's criminal!' Pauline laughs, rising. 'Your own stepson and you've never met. Please,' she reaches for Joanna's hand and squeezes it. 'He'd be so disappointed. Please wait here for a minute.'

Crossing the room, Pauline opens a doorway and leans through it. Beyond her, Joanna can make out a narrow carpeted hallway. 'Christopher,' she calls. 'Christopher?'

'Coming,' a voice answers.

Joanna stands stiffly, listening to footsteps approaching. When the door finally opens, Joanna hears her own gasp. The bag in her hand drops unceremoniously to the floor. Pauline is leading him towards her by the hand, saying her name, smiling. Christopher, Joanna thinks. Christopher, Christopher. The tall man grins, his white hair catching the light. 'Robert,' she begins to say, but the word lodges in her throat.

'This is my son,' Pauline is saying somewhere far away. 'Joanna?'

'Yes,' Joanna says, staring at him. 'Christopher.'

'Christopher,' Robert confirms, smiling. He leans forward and kisses her fondly, familiarly, on her cheek. 'I can't tell you how pleased I am to see you again.'

She shakes her head. 'I don't understand,' Joanna manages.

Christopher takes her hands in his own, his face tender, almost, Joanna thinks, paternal. 'You should share my faith in fate,' he says kindly. 'Fate and destiny, remember?'

'Yes,' Joanna says, slowly beginning to smile.

'Well,' she hears Pauline sit and pour herself another cup of tea, 'now that we've all been properly introduced, we have some things to discuss.'

'We do?' Joanna says. Christopher, still holding her hands, pulls her down to sit beside him on the other couch.

'Some important things,' Pauline continues, as if she hasn't heard. 'I think, Joanna, it's time for us all to consider our respective positions. Now let's just see,' she smiles, 'if there isn't a way for us to help each other. More tea, my dear?'

Chapter Thirty

'Well,' she laughs, 'and how was the artist's colony up north?'

He grins at her, clasping her hand. Pauline has tactfully left them alone in the apartment, claiming another appointment. For hours the three of them have been locked in conference, pooling their information, setting their objectives, making their plans. Joanna feels flushed with energy and power. For the first time in her own recent memory, she has something important to do.

'Just fine,' Christopher says. 'I thought of you.'

'You did?' She asks, pleased.

'I even painted you, my memory of you.'

'Oh God,' Joanna flushes, 'not tied up in a closet, I hope?'

He laughs fondly. 'No,' Christopher says. 'Wait here.'

She watches him rise and leave the room. The late afternoon sun darkens in shadow across the Persian rug, and Joanna knows she will have to leave soon. She dreads the ride home to the suburbs, the simple, immaculate meal Curtis will prepare, the simple-minded chatter he will expect of her. She helps herself to another cup of tea, now cold in the silver teapot.

Christopher returns, carrying a stiff piece of board. 'For you,' he says. 'I want you to have it. It isn't signed, for obvious reasons.'

Joanna takes the painting, a sweet watercolor of herself, reclining in her white strapless bathing suit on the pale sand, the ocean stretching before her in beautiful colors. 'How lovely,' she says. 'This is how you think of me.'

'Yes,' he confirms. 'Just before you woke up. I could see all of it in your sleep, the passion inside you, and the innocence. I thought you were the most beautiful woman I'd ever seen.'

Joanna blushes. 'Thanks,' she says, leaning over to kiss him. He takes her head in his hands and offers her his tongue. Joanna sucks it, loving its curve, thinking longingly of the beautiful curve in his cock and wishing she could suck that. He draws away, panting.

'Mm,' Christopher smiles. 'There's so much time. Afterwards, I mean.'

'Yes,' Joanna nods.

'But I do want you,' he tells her.

'I know,' Joanna says, kissing his nose. He leans back against the cushions and sighs happily.

'I guess you can tell me now,' Joanna says. 'About your hair. Your hair turning white, I mean.'

He nods, his eyes closed. 'Yes,' Christopher says. 'Dear Daddy.'

'Curtis?'

Christopher chuckles. 'The same. We were living in another apartment then, farther downtown along the park. Mother was away. I was in school and I ate some sordid thing for lunch and got sick, so they sent me home in a cab. When I got there, I heard sounds in the bedroom. Squealing. I thought my father was having another heart attack so I raced in, and there he was.'

'There he was,' Joanna repeats glumly, guessing the rest.

'He was spread-eagled on the bed. Tied up. With some ludicrous thing sticking out of his ass and a woman letting him have it with a riding crop. I nearly died.' Christopher shakes his head, remembering. 'I threw up on the spot. Then Dad started screaming and I promptly fainted. When I woke up, it was two days later, and I was in the hospital.'

'And your hair was white,' Joanna concludes.

'And my hair was white,' he says.

She pauses, thoughtful. One hand reaches out to touch it, stroke it between her fingers. 'Did your mother know?' Joanna asks quietly.

He shakes his head. 'She hadn't known. But I told her, of course. They got divorced the following year.' He laughs to himself. 'I guess it inspired her, because 'O' was born almost as soon as she was living apart from him. And over the years he got a little bolder and called her up, and she started looking after him, as a client.' He pauses. 'She's been waiting a long time for this, Joanna.'

Joanna nods. 'I know. I can tell.' She leans forward and nuzzles the white hair away from Christopher's ear until she can speak directly into it, into his heart. 'I'm going to get him for you too,' she says.

Chapter Thirty-One

Slowly the summer progresses, growing into a dense and humid August. Increasingly, Joanna's life begins to revolve around her Tuesdays and Thursdays in the city, the subtle unfolding of her own revenge, Pauline's revenge, Christopher's revenge. Here, she feels, she is free to meet with her husband for the first time as a whole and ironically honest self, and to meet him in his most honest incarnation: open to pleasure, pain, negotiation, humility. A truly naked intimacy, Joanna thinks. And an unexpected satisfaction.

Often, even when she is not in the chamber, Joanna spends her time thinking of that empty room, its possibilities and potential. She devises torments for her husband, small offerings of pleasure, instructions, punishments, combinations of restraint and freedom. At home in the evenings he continues to be infuriatingly gentle, concerned, devoted. Joanna exudes sweetness over the dinner table, chattering on about art, her class, her latest attempt at a still life or a landscape. Curtis swells with maddening fondness. She goes, seething, into his arms.

There are no more phone calls between the house in the suburbs and the penthouse overlooking the park. Indeed, it is regrettable that there are any, permanently recorded on some piece of paper in the bowels of the phone company. But no one is especially worried about the situation. After all, it's hardly unheard of for a husband to keep in touch with his wife of so many years, especially given the fact that they had a child together. There is nothing, in the end, to firmly connect Curtis to 'O'. 'O' itself is underground. No documentation, except for a small collection of business cards, exists to confirm it. Its transactions are restricted to telephone conversations and cash. Its phone is listed as private. Its profits disappear into a numbered account, hidden beneath the cobbled streets of Zurich. Its employees and clients guard it from outside attention. It is in many ways, as Mr. Stephens (who is so fond of secrets) has said, the best kept secret in the city.

The apartment on the west side of the park is technically owned by a corporation which, upon further examination, consists of Curtis himself. Expensive soundproofing has dispensed with the problem of curious neighbors, and the brownstone, in any case, tends to be rather deserted during the day. As does the street itself. It is, quite plausibly, a place retained for his own use and which he regularly uses, either with company or, quite often, alone. And Curtis's will, safe in Mr. Stephens' vault, leaves nothing to Pauline anyway, a situation agreed to and contracted for in their divorce settlement.

Where is the motive? Everything goes to Joanna. Everything, that is, except a thoughtful gift to Mr. Stephens and a generous bequest to Christopher. An apology of sorts, Joanna thinks. An apology for his beautiful white hair.

Curtis had had one heart attack before the day Christopher found him at the mercy of his mistress, and upon being discovered by his son, he dutifully had another, ironically realizing the fears that had made Christopher open the door in the first place. He had a third heart attack only months before his marriage to Joanna, but chose to tell her nothing about it, nothing about the previous one, nothing about the one before that. He is so fragile, Joanna now understands. And despite his own claims, he surely *is* past his prime, well past it, unforgivably past it. But still he subjects himself to the stress of his sexual needs, his desire for humiliation and punishment, driven by something so deep within himself that it carries the force of demand over reason. Such secrets, Joanna thinks, shaking her head, such powerful secrets. And now they are all hers.

Chapter Thirty-Two

He waits for her in the corner, hooded, obedient.
She makes him bend for the whip, spreading himself
open to her without dignity, then she punishes him
for that with the whip, with the rough violation of
her fingers, with her own, palpable disgust. Joanna
torments him, goads him, makes him ricochet
between promises and threats. Her punishment is
frenzied.

She makes him stretch and bend until he is
exhausted. He visibly sags as Joanna's watch
approaches four o'clock. She forces him to brace

himself against the walls, to grab the surfaces of the room, to turn the pages of the pornographic magazines she brings him, even though he can't see the pictures, just to cover them with his fingerprints. As for herself, Joanna has been wearing leather gloves to her meetings with Curtis ever since her conversation in the penthouse, wiping the surfaces in the apartment, anything she might ever have touched, anything Rochelle might ever have touched. She thoroughly scrubs the bathroom, removing every stray hair from the drains and then, after the session is over, gathering strands of Curtis's hair and plastering them to the toilet and sink and bathtub. She does not use the bathroom, herself. Gradually, she cleans out the drawers and closet of the rear bedroom, leaving plastic bags of leather, silk and lace in garbage receptacles around the Red Light district, where she knows, they will soon be discovered and recycled.

Increasingly, she forces him to masturbate to climax, filling the room with patches of drying semen like an animal marking his terrain. She brings him a large inflatable doll and commands him to fuck it, to pretend it is his wife so that she can watch him. Over and over he fills it with semen. She makes him push rubber phalluses into his own body, gradually working her way through the entire stock of them until they are all marked with him, his fingers, his secretions. She puts the whips into his hands, one by one, telling him to feel the length of them, the hardness, the thickness, imagine how much they will hurt when she uses them against his skin. He moans in anticipation as she takes them back, into her gloved hands. Joanna no longer wears a scent of any kind. The air inside the chamber reeks of sex and shame.

Sometimes, when she has finished beating him, he collapses in weariness at her feet, breathing hard. She stands over him, her crotch to his face, and lets him lick her in apology for his disobedience. His mouth is tender, poignant. Joanna stands, letting herself wash over with pity, absentmindedly stroking his head through the leather. She is not, after all, without regret, but her regret is for what might have been, not what was. The mouth at her cunt, the scarred, exhausted body at her feet, is part of a past already dimmed by the glorious promise of her future, a future she wants as she has never wanted anything before. That's good, she tells him, murmuring, stroking his head and rubbing herself softly against him. He sucks, straining to please her and she moans for him because it isn't hard to moan and it won't be much longer now, in any case. Not much longer.

Chapter Thirty-Three

'Finally!' he says, smiling at her across the dinner table. 'I'm delighted. I haven't wanted to push you, of course. I didn't want you to feel you had to show me your work before you were ready, but I'm very excited to see it.'

'Good,' Joanna tells her husband. 'Wait here. I'll bring it down.'

'Wonderful.' Curtis pours himself another glass of wine.

Joanna goes upstairs to her bedroom and takes Christopher's small watercolor from a drawer in her bedside table. The simplicity of the picture belies its skill, and Curtis, despite his self-proclaimed knowledge of art, will almost certainly see it as the work of a talented amateur. She takes it downstairs and places it in his hands. Then she resumes her seat at the table.

'Well,' Curtis says, nodding slowly. He holds the picture delicately, braced between his palms, careful not to mar it with his fingers. Slowly, he smiles, his lips pursing. 'Well, this is just lovely.'

'Thank you,' Joanna says. 'Do you really like it?'

'It's beautiful,' Curtis tells her. 'You're really very talented, do you know that?'

'You really think so?' She asks, excited, hanging on his approval.

'Of course. I must say, I'm very impressed. These colors, here in the ocean, and you here in your bathing suit. Just lovely.' He pauses. 'And this is how you see yourself.'

'I suppose,' Joanna says absently. 'Well, I mean, I wasn't thinking of seeing myself in any particular way. I just painted myself at the beach, you know? Why? How do you think I look?'

'Oh . . . soft. And pure. And very sweet. Just as you are,' he smiles. Curtis studies the picture again. 'It isn't signed, you know.'

'Well,' Joanna smiles, 'I didn't feel right about that. I mean signing it like a real artist, you know.'

'Why ever not?' He says. 'This is a real painting, and you made it. That makes you a real artist.'

She blushes. 'I suppose.'

He smiles tenderly at her. 'Will you sign it now?'

'All right,' Joanna says. 'I'll sign it to you. You can keep it if you like. Maybe in your bedroom.'

'Yes,' Curtis says. 'Thank you darling. That would be lovely.'

He hands Joanna a pen and she takes the painting from him, signing in the lower right hand corner. 'For my darling husband,' she writes, 'who inspired me to become an artist. I love you, Joanna.'

'Oh how sweet,' he tells her when she passes it back to him. 'Thank you.'

'Thank *you*,' Joanna says.

Curtis smiles down at the painting in his lap. 'It's funny,' he muses. 'It reminds me of something. Some of the paintings my son used to do, when he was younger.'

'Really!' Joanna says. 'You didn't tell me your son was an artist.'

'He was,' Curtis says dismissively. 'I don't know if he is anymore.'

Joanna pauses, letting the subject rise between them. 'You've never told me much about your son,' she says quietly. 'You said his name was Christopher, right?'

'Right,' Curtis nods, his eyes on the painting. 'We haven't spoken in many years. Almost fifteen, I think.'

Joanna frowns. 'But darling, why?'

He shrugs. 'We were never very close,' he says, 'and then we had a bit of a falling out, when he was a teenager.'

'How strange.' Curtis says nothing. 'Over what?' Joanna asks.

'Oh,' he sighs, 'the usual, I suppose. The usual reasons teenage sons fall out with their fathers. I didn't get along with my own father, after all. I didn't respect him. He was such a slave to mother. Anyway . . .' Joanna watches, silent, hoping Curtis will continue. 'Anyway,' he goes on, 'I've actually been thinking about Christopher lately, wondering if I should get in touch with him again. You know,' he smiles at Joanna, 'since you've come into my life I feel so peaceful about everything. Perhaps I'm capable of mending bridges now. After all, I'm a much different man than I was fifteen years ago.'

'Of course,' Joanna murmurs.

'I'm not even sure where he lives now,' Curtis says, laying the painting down on the table and reaching for Joanna's hand. 'But sometimes I think about him and wish I could see him.'

'My darling,' Joanna smiles. 'You are such a sweet man.' She leans forward, confiding. 'You deserve everything you want, and if this is what you wish for, I know you will get your wish.'

Chapter Thirty-Four

The last Thursday in August dawns steamy and hot. Joanna, tense with anticipation, rides the sweltering train into the city and takes a taxi uptown to a department store near the park. In a bathroom off the frenzied cosmetics floor, she changes into a short dress, black and clinging, and fits her black wig over her own blond hair. Lingering near the sinks, she surreptitiously collects fallen hairs: red, brunette, bleached blond and Asian black. She puts them carefully into her bag. Then folding the modest suburban dress she had worn on the train into her bag, she takes another taxi to an address a few blocks away from the apartment. Slowly she drifts through the empty streets, sluggish in the moist heat. Casually, Joanna winds her way to the brownstone, then smoothly climbs the steps and lets herself in.

Christopher is already there, seated on a chair by the window in the rear bedroom, wearing a tight woolen cap over his white hair. Smiling, he gets to his feet when she enters and hugs her tightly, his cheek pressed to hers. 'You ready?' He says softly. Joanna nods.

Together, they move through the apartment, both gloved, inspecting it with cautious eyes. Beneath the row of mounted whips, Christopher finds a long blond hair that has somehow slipped from beneath her wig. He hands it, smiling, to Joanna, who puts it carefully into the plastic bag she carries. He finds another near the black bureau, and she finds a blond pubic hair beneath the low table, both of which disappear into the plastic bag. When they are finished, Joanna hands Christopher the collection of hairs she has brought from the department store, and he carefully begins to spread them around the room, plastering them to whips, letting them fall to the surface of the black bureau, embedding them in the carpet. When they are finished, Joanna stands with her hands on her hips and looks slowly around the chamber. Involuntarily, she shivers.

'Second thoughts?' Christopher says quietly. Joanna shakes her head.

'No. Just nerves. Will you know when to come in?'

'I think so,' he nods. 'I'll be listening. Are you all right?'

'Yes,' Joanna says, meeting his gaze. 'I hate him, you know.'

'I know,' Curtis smiles. 'And that is only one of the many things we have in common.'

'Yes,' she says. At that moment, they both hear the front door open. Joanna gestures towards the rear bedroom, and silently they leave the chamber.

The wait is tense, and seems impossibly long. They hear him undress, the drape of his clothing over the back of the chair, two taps as his shoes fall to the floor, then the rustle of his silk underwear sliding on. A door clicks open then shut. The shuffle of feet across the black carpet next door. A preparatory moan. Then silence. Joanna takes an armload of the pornographic magazines Curtis has already marked, blows a kiss to Christopher, and enters the chamber.

Curtis stands in his customary place against the wall. The leather over his head shines black in the dim light. Joanna sees the evidence of their past sessions, colonies of healing welts across the backs of his thighs. Beneath his underpants, she knows, are many more, all in various stages of healing. Today, however, there will be no new welts, no cuts, no punishment requiring the presence of another human being in this room. Today, Curtis will punish himself, and suffer with his own self-inflicted wounds. She quietly scatters the magazines around the room, letting him hear the rustle of paper, then softly paces the carpet behind him for a long moment, before she speaks. When she does, at last, her husky foreign voice vibrates through the fetid room.

'Turn around,' Joanna says. 'Get down on your knees, your head on the floor.'

Curtis obediently kneels and bends, his shoulder-blades trembling. Joanna sits in a chair, a few feet away.

'I have been thinking about you,' she tells him quietly. 'I have been thinking a great deal about your disobedience, and my own attempts to make you good. It is very clear that my previous, gentle approach has had no effect on your behavior, isn't it?'

'Yes, Mistress,' he says, cringing.

'I have tried to make you good, but you continue to disobey. I am very sorry to tell you that I have decided to punish you severely. This is for your own good. You are my slave, and unless you can be good, I will be forced to terminate you. Do you understand?'

'Yes, Mistress,' Curtis sighs. 'I'll try harder. I'll try to be good.'

'Of course you will,' she agrees. 'You will have to. My patience with you has run out. I am quite prepared to kill you if you displease me further. Do you understand?'

'Yes,' he moans.

'Then come here. Crawl.'

He crawls forward, blindly, his head close to the ground. When he draws near, Joanna stops him with her boot against his leather hood. 'Lick it,' she says quietly. 'Lick my feet.'

He licks enthusiastically and she listens silently to the smacking of his tongue. 'You're so bad,' Joanna croons, giving him her other boot to lick. 'You're so very bad. You've done bad things, terrible things. Haven't you?'

'Yes,' Curtis groans between licks.

'And now you have to be punished for them, and it's so very sad. So sad, but I have to do it, don't I?'

'Yes, Mistress,' he says, his voice constricted. Joanna imagines him starting to cry inside the leather mask.

'What is the worst punishment you can imagine?' She asks him softly. 'What is the most terrible thing I can do to you?'

'The whip,' he sighs longingly, and she shakes her head smiling grimly.

'Worse than the whip, worse than anything you can dream of. I am going to hurt you so deeply.'

'No,' he moans, ecstatic.

'Stand up,' Joanna says.

He gets awkwardly to his feet. She takes her husband's wrist in her gloved hand and leads him slowly across the room to the edge of the low table. 'Pull down your pants,' she whispers, her voice seductive at his ear. Curtis does, easing the silk over his erection. It throbs at attention when he releases it, the scrotum tight behind it. 'Ooh,' Joanna croons, touching him briefly. The cock jerks when she makes contact. 'Aren't you hard?'

'Yes,' Curtis says.

'I've never seen you so hard,' she breathes. 'Does it hurt to be so hard?'

'Yes,' he moans. 'It hurts.'

'It makes me hungry,' Joanna confides, her voice low. 'It makes me want to be fucked, so deep and so hard. Does it make you want to be fucked?'

'Oh yes. It makes me want to be fucked.'

'That's good,' she croons, 'because you're going to be fucked. You're going to fuck yourself, and I'm going to watch you do it.'

'No,' he groans. 'No, Mistress, please.'

She reaches between his legs and swiftly pinches his scrotum, making him jerk with pain, telling him to shut up, then she pushes him down to sit at the edge of the low table. 'Spread your legs,' she hisses. He does.

Joanna goes to the wall and takes down the largest whip in the collection. It is a bullwhip, thick and stiff at its handle with a long trailing tail. Joanna cracks it experimentally over Curtis's head and he moans in anticipation. Crossing the room, she takes a tube of lubricant from the top of the bureau, delicately unscrewing the cap and dropping it on the carpet. She places the handle of the whip in Curtis's palm and closes his fingers around it. He shudders.

'Feel it,' Joanna moans. 'Isn't it thick? Think how it's going to feel, fucking you.'

'No,' Curtis whispers. 'God, no.'

She puts the tube of lubricant in his other hand and squeezes it, guiding the gel onto the leather handle. 'Rub it,' she sighs in his ear. 'Get it as hard as you are. Get it ready to fuck you.'

Joanna takes the squeezed tube away, careful not to smear the marks he has made on its surface. Curtis strokes the whip handle, softly at first and then with a firm grasp, coaxing its imaginary erection. 'That's good,' Joanna croons, watching him. 'It's so hard for you now, isn't it?'

'Yes,' he moans, and she smiles.

'Then fuck yourself, you piece of shit.'

Groaning, Curtis pushes the handle of the bull-whip into his rectum. His head falls back in pain. Inches disappear inside his body. She pushes his shoulders back onto the table and his hands slowly retreat from the leather, resting on his thighs. Joanna reaches beneath the table and brings up the leather straps, placing them in his palms. 'Strap yourself in,' she instructs him. 'Tight.' He fumbles with the buckle, smearing the metal with lubricant, slipping it into place and tightening it until it is snug across his ribcage. Curtis' erection is throbbing now, and Joanna presses it lightly between her gloved fingers, making it leap. He moans into the leather mask. She takes one of his hands, still sticky with the clear gel, and places it over his cock, telling him to stroke himself and he does, as if it were the whip he has just masturbated into hardness and plunged into his own body. Joanna carefully twists the bullwhip, moving it inside her husband's rectum, covering his moans with her own.

'Doesn't it feel good?' She croons, watching him inch closer to his climax. She creeps around the table, kneeling near his head. 'Isn't it good?'

'Yes,' he gasps, his head rolling.

'And you're going to come, aren't you?'

'Yes,' Curtis moans. 'Please, yes.'

'And who do you think of when you come?'

'You.' His hands quicken. 'You, Mistress.'

'No.' Her own, natural voice is suddenly cold at his ear. 'You think of your wife. You think of Joanna. Because Joanna is watching you right now.'

Abruptly, the hands freeze in mid-stroke. Curtis's mouth, visible through the hole in his leather hood, is open, stiff with shock. Joanna watches the disbelief crust over his body like a mist of sweat. 'It's impossible,' he whispers, barely aloud.

'Oh no,' she smiles. 'How could it be impossible, sweet Curtis? I'm here right now, watching you come with a bullwhip sticking out of your ass.'

'Joanna!' He gasps. 'Oh my God. Oh Christ, Joanna!'

'Don't stop,' she whispers. His hands are motionless, gripping his cock. She places her hands over his and squeezes gently.

'Oh my God,' Curtis moans. 'No, Jesus.'

'And I'm not alone,' she whispers, gripping him. She reaches down to gently nudge the whip into his bowels. 'I've brought your son. I've brought Christopher to see you. You said how much you wished to see him, and I want to please you, my darling Curtis, so he's here. He's home early from school, Curtis. He doesn't feel well. He's closing the front door behind him, can you hear it?'

In the rear bedroom, the bathroom door shuts loudly.

'No!' Curtis screams, 'Joanna!'

'Yes,' she hisses, 'he hears you screaming. He's afraid you're having another heart attack. *Are* you Curtis?'

'No!' He shouts, trying to sit up. The leather strap at his chest stops him. He tries to move his hands from underneath Joanna's but she grips him fiercely with unsuspected strength. 'God, help me!'

'He's worried about you,' Joanna says flatly. 'He hears you moaning and screaming. He runs to the bedroom door. Can you hear him?'

There is a sharp knock, the turn of a handle. Then silence. Curtis's chest heaves, gulping for air.

'And there you are!' Joanna shouts. 'Tied up on the bed with a rubber cock up your ass, and he sees you. He sees you, doesn't he?'

'Please,' he wheezes, 'Not . . .'

The door clicks shut. 'Daddy,' Christopher gasps. 'My God, what are you *doing*!'

Abruptly, Curtis bucks in pain beneath the leather strap. Joanna holds onto his hands. He kicks wildly, his body shot through with panic, jerking and heaving. She hears the primal sounds of violent death, death from disbelief, death from fear. Even, she thinks, death from shame. Perhaps this is what it means to die from shame. Curtis stiffens, the contractions easing. She feels something wet flow over her fingers and sees, to her surprise, that her husband has actually climaxed while in the act of dying. Or possibly, it is the other way around. Joanna smiles, releasing him. The semen drips slowly onto the carpet. There is something sweet in that, she thinks. The ultimate pain and the ultimate pleasure: an appropriate finale.

Chapter Thirty-Five

Christopher reaches for his father's wrist and holds it gently, checking for a pulse. After a minute, he gets to his feet, releasing the limp hand. 'Goodbye, Daddy,' he says, softly, without irony. He looks up at Joanna and smiles. 'Not a bad way to go.'

'It looked pretty bad,' she says doubtfully, and he shrugs.

'Not if you consider that he's courted this for years.

'Yes,' she sighs.

'Are you okay?'

Joanna nods. Christopher steps over to her and hugs her, his arms over hers. She relaxes against his shoulder and closes her eyes.

Later, they make a final sweep through the apartment, checking for anything that might have been left behind in the rear bedroom. The scene in the chamber is dramatic: whips and chains, scattered pornographic magazines, the repulsive, oft-used inflatable doll languishing in a corner, squeezed tubes of lubricant on the floor and, in the center of it all, a distinguished businessman, hooded, strapped onto a table with a long bullwhip protruding from between his legs, one hand stuck to his cock with lubricant and drying semen.

'Pretty ignoble,' Joanna comments.

Christopher nods. 'At least he won't have to live through his own disgrace.' He looks at her. 'I think we're ready to go. Do we have everything?'

Yes, she nods. They turn the doorknobs delicately with their gloved hands, careful not to smear Curtis's fingerprints on the brass, setting the lock inside before they pull it closed behind them. Out on the landing, they stand for a long moment in silence. 'I'll go first,' Christopher says. 'Wait about five minutes.'

She gives him her gloves and he puts them in his bag, then leans over to kiss her. 'We'll see each other as soon as it's safe,' he whispers. Then he smiles. 'You're a very rich woman. I'll have to take you on proper, expensive dates.'

'I'm worth it,' Joanna tells him.

'I know,' he says. 'Goodbye.'

Joanna watches him walk down the stairs, then waits to hear the heavy click of the street door. When it comes, she counts slowly to one hundred and leaves herself, walking slowly outside and back into the steaming heat of the afternoon. She finds a taxi quickly, a few blocks from the apartment, and crawls through traffic to the art museum on the other side of the park. There is a huge exhibition of work by a radical male photographer, recently deceased. Whips and chains are featured prominently, and the proper, leisured women of the city walk stiffly past the work, their faces set. Joanna smiles to herself. In the bathroom, she changes back into her own more modest dress and removes her black wig, stuffing it deep into the paper towel receptacle and covering it with wadded towels. Then she leaves the museum and hails another taxi to the train station.

It is nearly six by the time Joanna arrives home. The little house is snug and welcoming in the fading light. Joanna opens a bottle of Curtis's best wine and takes it outside to drink on the porch, relishing its color, its coolness, its sweet slide down her throat. The water laps gently at their small patch of rocky shoreline. She watches the swoop of seagulls, and suddenly wishes she really were able to paint because she would like very much to paint this moment and remember it forever, her own sense of release and happiness, the intense satisfaction of her revenge.

It's a good thing she's had experience as an actress, Joanna thinks. There is some difficult work ahead. Soon, she will call Curtis' office: concerned, reluctant to bother anyone but, well, just wondering if her husband was there, by any chance. Oh, well, he'll probably be home soon, silly of her. She sighs, smiling.

Then, soon after that, one or two friends. Trevor, perhaps. He wouldn't have any idea where Curtis was? Oh, it's just that he was late and she was worried, just overreacting, as usual, forgive her.

Then the police: cautious, apologetic. It's probably nothing but her husband is never this late without calling and she's worried and, well, will they at least make a note of his name and call her, please call her, here is the number. And the hospitals, to check, to leave his name and her own. Then the police again, increasingly panic-stricken, hysterical.

Afterwards, when she has placed him on file as a Missing Person, a period of terror, then resignation, bafflement until the body is discovered, which may take some time since no one but Curtis and 'O' know about the apartment. Someone will smell something bad, very bad. The police will be called. An unknown corpse will be found in a most scandalous condition. Shock, when she is notified. An absolute refusal to believe that this is Curtis, her own sweet Curtis, then the gradual slide into conviction. His clothing, his wallet, his teeth, his fingerprints smeared all over the room, marking grotesque instruments of torture and bondage and self-abuse. Her mortification when meeting with his friends and colleagues. Their whispered speculation about her own sex life with Curtis. Tasteless newspaper articles, ruthless television journalists waiting at her front gate to catch a voyeuristic glimpse of the devastated widow. Her insistence that the police pursue even the remotest possibility that Curtis wasn't alone when it happened, and then, her gradual, reluctant acceptance of the fact that he was. A funeral, memorial services, the reading of the will in Mr. Stephens' office, aching to reach out and touch Christopher who is seated only a few feet away. Yes, Joanna thinks. It's a good thing she has experience as an actress.

She checks her watch. It's getting late, and soon she will need to begin, but not quite yet. There is time for another glass of wine and another toast to the cornerstone of the life she is soon to begin leading. Happiness and wealth, Joanna thinks, raising her crystal goblet to the setting sun. And many long leisurely afternoons to spend with her new friends in the city.